A True Test
For Skye

Other Books in the Keystone Stables Series

KEYSTONE STABLES

BOOK 2

A True Test for Skye

by
Marsha Hubler

Zonderkidz

Zonder**kidz**.

The children's group of Zondervan

www.zonderkidz.com

A True Test for Skye
Copyright © 2004 by Marsha Hubler

Requests for information should be addressed to:
Grand Rapids, MI 49530

Library of Congress Cataloging-in-Publication Data

Hubler, Marsha, 1947–
  A true test for Skye / Marsha Hubler.– 1st ed.
    p. cm.— (Keystone Stables)
  The love of her foster parents, her friend Morgan, and her own devotion to the horses and dogs at Keystone Stables help Skye become a Christian and to, in turn, find a way to help her troubled friend Sooze.
  ISBN 0-310-70573-8 (softcover)
  [1. Foster home care—Fiction. 2. Horses—Fiction. 3. Christian life—Fiction. 4. Friendship—Fiction. 5. Death—Fiction.] I. Title.
PZ7.H86325Ts 2004
[Fic]—dc22
                                                    2003018718

Special thanks to the Glupker family for the use of their ranch.

Editor: Barbara J. Scott
Interior design: Susan Ambs
Interior illustrations: Lyn Boyer
Art direction: Laura Maitner
Cover design: Gayle Raymer
Photography: Synergy Photographic

Printed in the United States of America

---

05 06 07 /❖DC/ 4 3 2

IN MEMORY OF

Beth Barnhart

who lost her battle with a brain
tumor but won the victory on
October 30, 1999

KEYSTONE STABLES

Map of the Chambers' Ranch

Chapter One

$\int$ ooze, what do you think you're doing?" Skye Nicholson's voice rang out high and shrill. She leaned out Sooze's bedroom window, reaching toward her best friend who had staked herself out on the scorching-hot porch roof, a gallon can of kerosene in one hand and a cigarette lighter in the other. "Your mother called us. She said you were—"

"Get lost!" Sooze screamed. "I hate this dump! I hate the old lady! I hate everything! Who cares if I go up in smoke? Just get out of here—and leave me alone. I mean it, or this place goes up in flames!" Sooze flicked the lighter directly under the can.

Skye's attention darted to Eileen Chambers, Skye's foster mother, standing in the front yard, staring up at them. "Sooze, please come down. Your mother is going to call the police if you don't," she said, her voice filled with concern.

Skye pulled herself back into the bedroom and hurried her sweating hands through her long, silky dark hair. Her brown eyes glanced around Sooze's ransacked room. *What will get her in from that roof?* Skye focused on a picture hanging lopsided on the wall, and then she took a deep breath. *Maybe, just maybe!*

Skye leaned out toward Sooze. "Hey, put that stupid lighter down, would ya? What do ya think that's going to accomplish anyway—besides getting you in even more trouble?"

"You think I care? What have I got to lose?"

"Maybe more than you think, Sooze. I was just going to talk to you about this great idea I had. You like horses, right?"

For a brief moment, the tiniest spark of hope flashed across Sooze's face, and she flicked the lighter off. Wiping sweat from her brow, she hunkered down against the side of the house, kerosene can and all.

Skye leaned out the window a little further to see if Sooze was listening. As usual, Sooze's chopped off, straight, mousy brown hair stuck out all over, especially where a cowlick crowned her head. Her dark hollow eyes and tight lips did nothing to enhance her skinny shoulders and big hips. A yard sale T-shirt hanging on her scrawny frame gave the impression of a wet blanket on a coat rack. The rest of her, packed into tattered jean shorts and sneakers full of holes, added to the unmade-bed look that had become her trademark.

Although Skye and Sooze had never had classes together at Madison Middle School, the two had been friends for several years. Skye's memory taunted her: lots of stolen prescription pills. Anytime. And dirt cheap. Sooze had been Skye's supplier. At the time, it was easy to like anybody with a prize like that attached to the friendship. Thinking about it made Skye realize how much she'd changed.

Again, Skye yelled out to Sooze, "Don't go anywhere! I have to check on something, but I'll be right back to tell you about my idea."

"Yeah, right," Sooze said.

Skye raced out of the bedroom and down a hallway. Two and three at a time, Skye clattered down a flight of rickety stairs and came to an abrupt halt in the doorway of the kitchen. Sooze's mother, Mrs. Bodmer, sat at her kitchen table, feeding her nervous lips a cigarette and twiddling a can of cold beer. Her fingers, flaming with bright red polish, paraded as many rings as they could hold.

"I ain't never been able to control that kid since she was little," Mrs. Bodmer mumbled to herself, snuffing out her cigarette in an overflowing ashtray.

Skye bit her lower lip as Sooze's mother continued to ramble, now directing her diatribe toward Skye. "She just wouldn't listen, and now—*now*—she wants ta kill me! I don't know what I ever did to make her hate me! She hates me, you know, and—"

Skye turned to see Mrs. Chambers coming in the front door. Before she was halfway across the living room, Skye was at her side. "Hey," Skye said breathlessly. "I just remembered that Sooze loves horses. I only said the word 'horse' once, and she shifted her freak-out gear into neutral. Could I tell her she can come out to Keystone Stables and ride? I'm sure she doesn't really wanna burn the house down."

"Anything's worth a try at this point, Skye," Mrs. C. answered. "How's her mother holding up?"

They both glanced into the kitchen where Sooze's mom was lighting another cigarette, blowing puffs out of her nose like a steam engine ready to explode. Her bottle-blond, frizzed-out hair was blowing in all directions from a fan perched on the counter next to a pile of dirty dishes.

"I'll talk to Mrs. Bodmer, and you go back upstairs," Mrs. C. suggested.

Skye rushed up the stairs and stuck her head through the window opening onto the roof. "Okay Sooze, you've got to come in now. I've got the best news ever. Mrs. C. says you can go riding with me out at Keystone Stables. But you have to come in if you want to hear the rest."

A week later at the Chambers' home, Skye sat at the dining table with Mr. and Mrs. Chambers, Sooze, and Mrs. Bodmer. Morgan, another foster child, worked diligently in the adjoining kitchen, wheeling around in her wheelchair.

"Now, Mrs. Bodmer—" began Mr. Chambers.

"When do I get to ride?" Sooze directed her question to Skye.

"Shut your mouth, Susan, and let the man talk!" Mrs. Bodmer snapped. "Be polite for once in your life!"

"It's Sooze—S–o–o–z–e—if you don't mind!" she sassed back.

"And what's wrong with your God-given name? You were named after your dear Aunt Susan. I hate that name—*Sooze!*" Mrs. Bodmer angrily twisted the rings on her fingers. "You just don't like Susan because I do. Plain and simple!"

"I'd rather be named after a circus elephant," Sooze said. She slumped abruptly and stared at the table. "Susan. How *boring!*"

"How did you get the name Sooze?" Mr. Chambers asked, in an effort to bring things under control.

"This is *sooo* funny!" Skye giggled and glanced at Sooze. "Go on. Tell him."

Sooze hesitated for a moment, glared at her mother, but finally began to speak. "Chuck, you know, my older brother who lives in Kentucky now? He used to let me play in the ashes from our coal furnace when I was real little. He'd laugh his head off and sing 'Snoozy Sooze, needs a Jacooze.' He'd make me laugh even though I was covered in soot from the top of my head to my little toes. I'm pretty sure he was selling tickets to all his friends just to come and have a look. Pretty soon they all started calling me 'Sooze.' So here I am—Sooze, *not* Susan."

Skye studied Mrs. Bodmer whose best effort at killing Sooze with her looks soured the room. *And the judge says Sooze is the one who needs help!* Skye thought.

"That's a great story." Mr. Chambers laughed, brushing his straight brown hair back off his forehead. He drew his fingers down both sides of his tidy mustache while he looked first at his wife and then at Mrs. Bodmer. "Now, we have some important issues to discuss.

"I've asked Eileen, Skye, and Morgan to meet with us because we have no secrets here." He turned toward the kitchen where the wheelchair-bound girl with long, kinky red hair worked at the sink. "Morgan, would you please join us for a family conference?"

"Comin', Mr. C.," answered Morgan. She closed the dishwasher door before motoring to the gap between Mr. Chambers and Sooze's mother.

"Mrs. Bodmer, this is Morgan Hendricks. She's been with us almost four years now."

"Hi," Morgan said, her freckles dancing with her smile.

"Are you a foster kid too?" Mrs. Bodmer asked.

"Yep," Morgan replied. "And I love it here. This place was made for kids like me. There are ramps and special equipment all over the place. It's so cool."

"Okay—Sooze, we want you to understand exactly why you are here," Mr. Chambers said, folding his hands and looking directly at Sooze. "As you know, your mother feels she is no longer able to control your behavior. She has asked the court to place you in our care. The court ordered that you are to live here as our foster child, while you attend the Maranatha Treatment Center program.

"When do I get to ride?" Sooze asked again.

"Susan, will you—" Mrs. Bodmer started sharply.

"Tom," Mrs. Chambers interjected as she stood, "I'll make a pot of coffee. Mrs. Bodmer, would you like some?"

"Yeah," Sooze's mother said, her tone much lighter.

"Girls, how about some iced tea?" Mrs. C. asked.

"Sure," Skye and Morgan answered at the same time. Sooze simply nodded.

Mr. Chambers opened a file and shuffled papers, spreading them out before him. "Mrs. Bodmer, according to this court order, Sooze will be with us for at least a year in both the foster home and at Maranatha. Among her list of offenses, it appears that she's been hustling drugs. Were you aware of her *extracurricular* activities?"

"What do ya expect me to do about it!" Mrs. Bodmer said. "It's not like she listens to anything I say."

Everyone expected Sooze to respond to her mother's comment, but instead, she leaned forward and placed her hands on each side of her head.

"What's wrong?" Skye whispered. "Another headache?" Sooze nodded.

Mr. Chambers hesitated for a moment as his wife Eileen served iced tea to the girls. "Coffee will be ready in a minute," she said.

Mr. Chambers picked up another paper. "Sooze will have drug and alcohol counseling at Maranatha three times a week, along with group counseling. Eileen will see that she gets there in the summer. When school starts,

Sooze will ride a van with the other clients to the treatment center at three o'clock every afternoon. Then she'll come home with my wife and Skye. Although she won't be living with you for a year, Mrs. Bodmer, we want you to know you are welcome here anytime. Just call before you plan to visit to be sure we're home. Any questions so far?" He put the paper down and folded his hands.

"How much is this gonna cost me?" Mrs. Bodmer grumbled.

"Nothing," Mrs. Chambers answered, placing three cups of coffee down as she rejoined the group. "When a child is court ordered into our program, the expenses are covered by state grants and private donations."

"Good!" Mrs. Bodmer wiped her forehead. "I can't afford nothing like this place. I barely make ends meet now, you know, with the house and car payments and all."

"Yeah, and of course, beer and cigarettes," Sooze threw in.

"Cool it!" Skye jabbed Sooze in the ribs.

As if not hearing Sooze's remark, Mr. Chambers said to her, "Now concerning your responsibilities here. You'll be helping with barn chores, housecleaning, cooking, lawn work—all the skills you will need to manage your own home someday. You'll have your own bedroom. Skye will show it to you in a few minutes. Later, Eileen and I will give you a tour of the barn and introduce you to the horses. From what I've heard, we won't have to hogtie you to get you on a horse. If you're like Skye, I'm sure you'd rather sleep in the barn than in a bed. Anyhow, I would say in about two weeks, you should be adjusted to the daily regimen."

"But it's not all hard work," Morgan added. "We have lots of fun here. It didn't take me long to find out that after the work, there's always time for other things. *And*, we do get five megabucks a week for our chores. Then there's the basement loaded with a pool table, Ping-Pong, and all those video games. And don't forget about the horses!"

"Megabucks—great! And when do I get to ride?" Sooze's words slid out quickly.

Mrs. Bodmer scowled at her daughter. "Susan, you sound like your brain's stuck on horse, horse, horse. Can't you get that horse business out of your head? These people are sick of hearing that. Mind your manners and hush up!"

Skye studied Mrs. Bodmer. *She is so lame*.

"Sooze," Mrs. Chambers said softly, "you'll find out about megabucks soon enough, and you'll get to ride after you've settled in here. We've been discussing which horse would be best for you since you're a beginner, and Skye had a great idea. Tell her, honey."

Skye took one quick sip of iced tea. "We have six horses, and I figured Stormy, the Tennessee Walker, is one of the gentlest."

"Stormy?" Sooze's confusion was apparent. "You have a gentle horse named Stormy?"

"His name matches his color—not the way he acts," Skye said. "His color reminds everyone of a storm cloud. I think he's the one for you."

A smile enveloped Sooze's face. "It's no big deal if he's wild or tame. I can ride any kind of horse. Just get me on one, and I'll show you."

Skye rolled her eyes and thought, *Yeah, right!*

"All in good time," Mrs. Chambers said.

"Sooze, you don't just hop on a horse and take off," Morgan added. "Can you believe that I ride even though I can't walk? This cerebral palsy didn't keep me from learning to ride. But it doesn't happen by waving a magic wand. It takes tons of practice."

"You ride horses?" Mrs. Bodmer asked, scratching her head. "How do you get on?"

Mr. Chambers chuckled. "We lift her on, but after that, she's a riding maniac! You should see all her blue ribbons!"

"Skye and Champ already have a blue ribbon too!" Morgan said.

"But I practiced a zillion hours before even thinking about a horse show," Skye added.

"Well, sign me up for a blue ribbon," Sooze said. "I can ride too! Just wait and see."

"Susan!" Mrs. Bodmer bellowed. "What am I gonna do with her? She never did listen, and it doesn't sound like she's gonna start now."

Chapter Two

Sooze sat cross-legged on her bed with her arms wrapped around Tippy and Tyler, the Chambers' West Highland terriers. "I love horses, I love dogs, and I love this place, Skye."

Skye had plopped onto the same bed with Sooze and now studied the glow on her friend's face.

"This is so cool, Sooze. I mean, you oughta be locked up at Chesterfield with your record. I think the Chambers put in a good word for you. Even though some of their rules seem stupid, they really do care about us."

"Ever since you invited me to that party a while back, I've been scoping out this place. It is *too* sweet, even with all the rules. I can't wait to get on that horse." Sooze stared deep in thought. "On the other hand, living here will make it harder until school starts, but I, the Great Sooze, will do it. Get us pills, I mean. They do let us out of the cage once in a while, don't they? You know, like, to the mall, or movies, or the store. I have friends all over the place."

Change the subject, Skye told herself. *Get her off the pill thing.* "We do go to the mall and for groceries every week. You've already seen what that's like when you and Mrs. C. bought stuff for this room." Skye scanned the four walls. "Horse pictures, horse curtains, horse spread, horses everywhere! Something tells me you're into horses big time. So you already know we go to the mall. Then there's church."

"Church? I thought I'd croak when Mr. Chambers mentioned that the other day!"

"I thought no way at first, too, but it's really not so bad," Skye said as she leaned up against the headboard of the bed, clasped her hands behind her head, and straightened her legs. "The youth-group leader talks about all kinds of neat stuff. Last week he talked about dating. And about how we're not old enough yet."

Skye's thoughts drifted into space as she thought about Chad, who was in the Youth for Truth group, and then she refocused on Sooze. "Besides, Judge Mitchell said you gotta go to church. It won't kill you."

"That's a joke, Skye. I don't need church. I need to make a buy. You gonna help me get some pills or not? I'll cut you in on the profit."

"No way, Sooze."

"You chicken?"

"No, I am *so* not chicken, thank you. It's just that I've learned an awful lot living here. One thing I've learned is that I don't need happy pills to have a good time. I also don't like to lose control of this." Skye tapped her head.

"The last time I got high, Mr. C. landed in the hospital. He fell off Chief trying to stop me from taking Champ over a wall jump. If Mr. C. had died, I—I don't know what I'd have done." Skye ran her fingers through her hair and sighed. "And let me tell you somethin' else. I've been thinkin' about God."

"I don't wanna hear it."

"No—wait! Listen, I used to think God didn't exist until he healed Mr. C. from that head injury. At least I think he did. Now I'm thinkin' twice about this God stuff. Sooze, he *might* be real!"

"Yeah, and turtles *might* do back flips. Girl, what's up with you? You used to be so much fun, but I've seen you change in the last few months. Are they gettin' to you?"

"Nobody's *gettin'* to me, Sooze. I've just been trying to *get* my act together. I used to be so mad at my parents, whoever and wherever they are, that I was always angry. Maybe that's part of your problem, too. You're mad at the whole world."

"Don't be puttin' your stuff off on me, Skye." Sooze shriveled up her face. "The only people I'm mad at are my so-called mother and those know-it-all teachers at school. Truth is, I don't care about nothin' anymore. But this idea of yours—it sounded like fun, so I figured why not? Beats goin' up in flames, right? And then the way it turned out—living here—that's even better. Why not be as close to the horses—and dogs as—possible?" She kissed the dogs and hugged them tighter.

"You don't know the Chambers like I do," Skye said. "They have eyes in the back of their heads. You are *not* gonna get away with anything here. Trust me on this one."

"Watch me!" Sooze hissed.

"Yeah, I'll watch you being grounded like I was for breaking the rules. Then there's the biggest pain of all— no horse, no barn, nothing. It stinks. Believe me, I know!"

"What about all our barn chores that we absolutely have to do every day? Huh? What then? Huh? You can touch the horses then, can't you?" Sooze raised her eyebrows.

"Somebody else does your chores, even if it means Mr. or Mrs. C. They will *not* let you near that barn if you get grounded. You might as well be in jail."

"I guess I'll have to make sure I don't get caught," Sooze said, her face beaming with a devilish smile.

"Can I join the party?" Morgan said, as she motored up to the doorway. "Mrs. C. wants to feed Tip and Ty. Okay, guys. Lunch is served!"

As the dogs jumped from the bed and made a hasty exit, Skye looked Morgan's way and smiled. *Whew, am I glad you're here*, her face said.

Sooze's eyes lit up with surprise. "Hey, how did they know their food was ready?"

"Those dogs listen better than we do," Skye said.

"All you have to do is say the word 'lunch,' and they're history," Morgan said as she moved next to the bed.

"Hey, Morgan, get this," Skye said, "Sooze thinks she's gonna run her own show here. Wanna tell her different?"

"You are in for the surprise of your life," Morgan said, flipping back her red hair. "I remember how clueless I was when I moved in. But I figured it out soon enough. Grounding. Grounding. And more grounding. I thought I'd never see the outside world again."

Sooze sprawled out across the bed on her belly. "How do you get grounded when you're already *grounded* in that thing? It's not like you're gonna be runnin' away or stealin' a car or anything!"

"Hey, I can drive! I drive a special van the Chambers have for people like me. I just got my license." Morgan held up her clenched hands and blew on her fingernails. "But I wouldn't think of doin' anything as lame as stealing the van. The Chambers have been too good to me. And besides, it's just plain stupid! Being grounded is awful. You lose phone and computer privileges, and I love playing Battleship on the Internet." Morgan flipped the joystick on her wheelchair, sending it into a continuous slow rotation. "And as far as this *thing*, it's called a Jazzy, and it can do just about anything but fly. See?"

"That's pretty cool!" Sooze said with a patronizing smile. Then she put her hands on the sides of her head and dug her elbows into the bed.

"Another headache?" Skye asked.

"Yeah," Sooze groaned.

"Headaches?" Morgan brought her chair to a stop. "You oughta tell Mrs. C. Sounds like you need your head examined."

"Yeah, it's probably empty!" Skye giggled.

Sooze blinked her eyes a couple of times. "Mom says it's from me spending so much time freaking out. She says I'm a walking time bomb and when the headaches stop, I'll explode. So you two better cross your fingers and hope this thumping doesn't stop, or the whole place will be Soozified!" She giggled weakly and pressed her head tighter.

Skye raised both hands, fingers crossed.

"Hey, I know what we can do," Morgan said. She started to back out of the room. "We can all pray about it."

"Pray? Don't think so," Sooze snapped. "They don't last that long."

But Skye could tell her friend was in real pain. She promised herself to tell Mrs. C. about it.

"When do I get to ride?" Sooze asked Skye as they leaned up against the white fence that bordered the pasture. To their right, a poor excuse for a truck loaded with hay rattled its way on the dirt road. The hot July sun had already been up for two hours and now washed over the girls' faces, forcing them to shield their eyes with their hands.

"You know, Sooze, your momsy might not be right about a lot of things, but she's right on about you having your brain stuck on *horses*," Skye said. "You've only been here for two days. I'm sure Mr. and Mrs. C. have big plans for you today. But I think I know what's comin' first."

"Hey, I already know plenty about riding horses," Sooze protested. "I've ridden lots of times at carnivals, and I even went to a riding camp once. I got my way paid on some kinda grant through the school. I always rode this one neat pony, Sugar. We'd go around and around in the corral until they made me get off."

"Riding a pony in a corral or in a circle at a carnival is so *not* the same as riding well-trained registered horses like these," Skye said. "Stormy knows what to do in an open field, but do you?"

"Don't get all preachy," Sooze said. "I know what I'm doin'. You'll see."

"Yeah, you'll see," Skye snickered. "I'm bettin' you have a lot to learn."

"Hey, you two," Mr. Chambers yelled as he got out of the truck, slamming the squeaky door shut. "Let's get this hay loaded into the loft. Then we'll show Sooze more of her chores in the barn!" Mr. Chambers grinned slyly.

"Great," Sooze complained. "I can hardly wait."

"Yeah, they're nasty," Skye said, "especially muckin' out the stalls. But at least we're close to the horses. Come on. Let's do the hay-into-the-loft thing. Then I'm sure Mr. C. will saddle up the horses."

"What's muckin'?" Sooze asked suspiciously.

"You'll see soon enough," Skye answered with a sly smile.

For the next half hour, Mr. Chambers pitched hay bales from the truck to Skye and Sooze in the loft of the barn. The girls dragged one bale at a time into the back and pushed and pulled each one onto a huge stack that looked like gigantic toy blocks against the wall. Covered with hay shreds and dust, they finally placed the last bale and then hurried to join Mr. Chambers on the ground level at the horse stalls.

"Good job, girls," Mr. Chambers said, dusting himself off with his stained tan cowboy hat. "Maybe the next time you should wear long sleeves and jeans like I suggested." His mustache chuckled. "Hay dust makes you very itchy."

Maybe I like to itch! Skye sassed to herself. "Too hot for jeans," she said matter-of-factly.

"Well, at least you have your boots on, Skye. I guess you know what's coming."

"Yeah, I know," Skye said, grinning.

"Sooze, you need a good pair of cowboy boots," Mr. Chambers added. "But until we take you shopping, I don't want you to ruin your sneakers."

This oughta be good, Skye laughed to herself. "Sooze, over there against the wall are a couple of pairs of big rubber boots. Pick the right size and put them on over your shoes."

"What do I need them for? It's not snowin'," Sooze complained as she walked to the wall.

"No, but you'll wish it was when you see what we're gettin' ready to do," Skye said.

"Skye," Mr. Chambers said, walking away, "since Stormy is going to be Sooze's horse, how about you two starting with that stall. I'll work the other side of the barn."

"Right, Mr. C.," Skye said, as she pointed. "Sooze, get the pitchfork and shovel down from the wall hooks. I'll get the wheelbarrow, and a muckin' we will go."

"I'm getting a bad feeling about this," Sooze said, starting toward the boots.

"Come on. You'll love it!" Skye said, smiling. "Mucking, with a capital *M*, *is* the only gross part of this horse stuff. Every day we have to shovel you-know-what out of each stall. But it doesn't take long to become a champion pooper-scooper. Really, it's not that bad, especially when you love horses. It just gives us another chance to be near them. And this is super important."

Skye opened Stormy's stall and continued her instructions. "After mucking, we put a fresh layer of straw down every day. It's not only easier on this," she said, pointing to her nose, "but it's mega-important for the horses' hooves. If they get thrush from standing in this stuff for days, they can go lame. Thrush is an infection that eats away the bottom of their hooves. And it smells worse than a garbage can on a hot summer day. So we *gotta* do this. Got it?"

"Got it," Sooze said, as she shriveled up her face and held her nose. "When do I get to ride?"

"Tomorrow!" Mr. Chambers yelled from the other end of the barn. "After you get your boots."

Chapter Three

Sooze, you look like you're ready to jump out of your skin!" Skye sat on Champ, his sorrel coat gleaming in the sun, outside the training corral next to the barn. "It's finally your turn. Hey, where'd you get those jeans and fancy boots and that hard hat?"

"Yeah," Morgan kidded. "Looks like you're ready to go in the house and do some dishes." She positioned Blaze, her Quarter Horse mare, next to Champ.

"Very funny," Sooze said as she sat on the corral rail, waiting for Mr. Chambers to bring Stormy out of the barn. She fooled with the hard hat, trying to get it to balance evenly on her head. "I don't need this dumb thing."

"Girls, girls, have mercy on this poor child," Mrs. Chambers said as she walked next to Sooze and gently touched her on the back. "Sooze, you have to wear the hat. State regulations."

Sooze shrugged Mrs. Chambers' hand off.

I remember when I pulled away from Mrs. Chambers like that, Skye told herself. *Sooze, you don't know what you're missing—a real mother's love.* "Sooze can take anything we dish out. She's *t-o-u-g-h* with a capital *T*. Aren't you, Sooze?"

Skye studied Sooze, waiting for a response, but Sooze had focused on the barn. One of the doors slid open, and all eyes shifted.

Mr. Chambers walked out of the barn leading a charcoal gray horse with a long flowing mane and tail. The horse, dressed in a royal blue blanket and tan western saddle and bridle, glistened in the sun. Skye feasted on the beauty of the gorgeous creature and recalled having ridden Stormy only once.

"He's too big for me," Skye said to Champ as she patted him on the neck, "but you're just right, boy."

Morgan overheard Skye. "Stormy is a big guy," she said, "but he's as gentle as he is big. He oughta be a good match for Sooze."

"It's not Sooze I'm worried about," Skye said. "I don't think Stormy knows what *he's* in for. We might see him freak out for the first time in his life when Supergirl gets on him."

"Hey, watch it," Sooze answered back.

"Okay, Sooze," Mr. Chambers said, as he led Stormy into the corral and closed the gate. "You've mastered your grooming, saddling, and leading sessions. Now it's time for you to mount."

Sooze wasted no time jumping down off the fence and running toward the horse. "Finally!" she yelled, hard hat wobbling and new boots causing her to stumble.

"Whoa, slow down," Mr. Chambers said. "You don't want to spook him. Remember, I told you to approach a horse—any horse—cautiously. Now stroke his neck and let him see you. Talk to him—softly. Let him smell you, so he can prepare himself for 'The Great Sooze.'"

"Sooze, you sure you wouldn't rather be cleanin' your room?" Skye laughed, and Morgan joined in.

"Girls, stop it," Mrs. Chambers gently chided. "You're wasting your breath. Just sit back and enjoy the ride."

"One thing about Sooze," Skye said, "she's no chicken like I was on my first ride. I don't think she's afraid of anything."

"Hmm," Mrs. Chambers said. "That's not always good, especially when you're around such powerful animals."

"Hopefully, living here will help her get her act together," Morgan said. "At school she's on the Top Ten list of the wildest kids at Madison. Mrs. C., I think you've got an impossible mission with this one."

"Well, with God's help, we can and will help her. Mr. C. and I are praying for her, just like we prayed for both of you."

Yeah, Skye thought. *We'll see.*

"Up you go!" With a strong shoulder, Mr. Chambers launched Sooze onto the patient horse. Sooze leveled her wobbly hat while Mr. Chambers checked the length of each stirrup. "Now take the reins in one hand, and I'm going to hold on to the bridle. We'll walk around in this corral until you feel 'tall in the saddle' as they say. Maybe in a week or two you'll be able to take him out in the open field."

Sooze confidently adjusted her hard hat. "I can do that now! I know what to do. I've ridden lots a times."

"Sooze, tune in to Mr. C.!" Skye yelled from the sidelines. "He knows what he's talking about."

"Patience, Sooze," Mrs. Chambers added. "Patience."

"But I've done this before," Sooze complained.

Mr. Chambers walked to the front of the horse and held the bridle. "Sooze, now listen to me. You have *never* ridden a horse like this one. Believe me. This is a Tennessee Walking Horse. You have to know what you're doing to, let's say, make him *work* right. God made this breed different from all others."

Skye scrunched up her face. She could tell Sooze didn't want to hear it.

"Sooze, why do you think he's called a Tennessee Walker?" Mr. Chambers asked.

"Because he's too lazy to run!" she sassed. "Let's go!"

"No, we're going to wait until you calm down. A horse can read you like a book, even before you get on his back. As wired as you are, Stormy might give you a ride into the next county. Now just stroke his neck and release the reins while I tell you about walkers. This is part of your training."

"Oh, fine." Sooze pouted.

Mr. Chambers began. "Walkers don't trot, nor do they run like other horses. God gave them a running walk. Their diagonal legs work almost in unison, all four hitting the ground at a different time, maybe a second apart. Their back legs have tremendous overstride, which causes an even rocking-horse action when they speed up. Now, you won't feel that when Stormy walks slowly, but as soon as you squeeze your legs the right way, he will be off into the smoothest ride you've ever felt—as smooth as running water. You'll feel like you're riding on a cloud. But first, you have to learn how to get on board. You are sitting on a blue-ribbon show horse, Sooze. Don't forget that!"

"I won't. Let's go!"

"All right. Now we're going to walk slowly in this ring for a long time. I'll show you how to stop, turn, and back up, and you can practice mounting and dismounting. Even though he's over sixteen hands, once you can get your foot in the stirrup with ease, I think you'll be mounting without help from anyone. Ready?"

"Yessss!"

"Here we go," Mr. Chambers said. He stepped to the left side of Stormy and clicked his tongue.

"Ride 'em cowgirl!" Mrs. Chambers yelled.

"Hey, Sooze, the dishes are waiting!" Morgan joked.

"Good-bye, carnival ponies. Hello, Stormy!" Skye added.

Sooze's face glowed with delight as the trio circled the corral. Skye couldn't remember seeing her friend so happy in all the time she'd known her.

Skye sat in the dining room with Morgan and the Chambers during lunch break. Like a beaver chewing a log, she gnawed off a row of corn on the cob and took a large gulp of milk. "Mrs. C., could we go to the mall one day this week? I've got my eye on a new video game."

"Oh," Mrs. Chambers replied, "I thought you said last week you needed new shoes for church and special occasions."

"Nah, the shoes can wait. I gotta have this game. Can we go?"

Mr. Chambers swallowed a bite of his sandwich. "Now, Skye, don't you think you should budget some of your allowance for important things—like a pair of shoes? I just realized that lately we haven't discussed giving to the Lord. Have you been tithing? You haven't forgotten about giving that 10 percent, have you?"

I know now that God is real, but I'm sure he doesn't need my measly couple of bucks! A faint smile covered Skye's thoughts.

"No, I didn't forget," she grumbled.

"Good," Mrs. Chambers said. "Don't leave the Lord out of any part of your life, honey."

Morgan chomped on a potato chip. "I remember how hard it was for me to get into the habit of giving my tithe at first. But when I learned how God uses what we give to help others, I finally got into it. It's so cool to see how my money can be used to help missionaries or families in need. I get as much out of giving as those getting the help. And God promises special blessings to those who tithe. I read about it in the Book of Malachi, in the Bible. You'll see."

Wanna bet? Skye thought. "Whatever," she mumbled.

Mr. Chambers drained his glass of water and wiped his mustache with a napkin. "Hey, where did Sooze go? She's been gone quite awhile, and she hasn't finished her lunch."

"She said she had to use the bathroom," Mrs. Chambers said. "Skye, would you mind checking on her?"

"No problem."

Skye pushed back her chair and headed down the hallway, knocking on the closed bathroom door. There was no answer, so Skye knocked again. Finally, she peeked in. The bathroom was empty, and the window was wide open!

"Mrs. C.!" Skye yelled. "Sooze isn't in the bathroom, and the window's wide open!" Skye called out, running back into the dining room. "I'm sure she wouldn't run away. She likes this horse stuff too much."

Morgan had just pivoted her chair and was glancing out the sliding glass doors. "Hey—how did Stormy get out in the big field?"

Everyone turned to the window in time to see Sooze trying to mount from the far side.

Mr. and Mrs. Chambers jumped up from the table so fast they almost toppled their chairs and ran for the door. Skye was right behind them.

"And no hard hat!" Mr. Chambers bellowed. He slid the door open in one swift move and charged out. "Sooze, don't get on that horse!"

"She'll kill herself!" Mrs. Chambers said.

Skye ran toward the field with Morgan motoring along behind her.

As Mr. Chambers raced across the lawn, Stormy pranced in tight circles with Sooze already mounted on his back.

"Watch me now!" she yelled. "I'll show you I can ride!"

Mr. Chambers took one courageous leap toward the fence. "Sooze, stop!"

Stormy wheeled, and Sooze grabbed the horn with one hand and the reins with the other. She shoved her heels into the unsuspecting horse's belly. Hard!

"You idiot!" Skye screamed, running to the fence. "That's no play pony!"

"Sooze! Sooze!" Mrs. Chambers, out of breath at the fence, could not utter another word.

"Sooze!" Morgan yelled. "Stop!"

"Let's go, Stormy!" Sooze whooped. "Let's show 'em how it's done!"

Chapter Four

Every muscle in Stormy's powerful body tensed with the excitement of running like the wind. A kick that hard in such well-trained ribs meant only one thing: go fast!

In a split second, the horse broke into a fast gallop and tore along the fence with Sooze hanging on for dear life. Like a rag doll tied to the saddle, she bounced with every hoof that pounded the ground while pulling back hard on the reins. "Whoa! Whoa!" she screamed.

Mr. Chambers, balancing on the fence railings, reached but just missed Sooze as she flew by. "Turn him in a circle!" he yelled as he cleared the fence and ran after her.

"Sooze!" Skye and Morgan yelled together, eyes wide with alarm. "Turn him in a circle!"

Stormy rounded the corner, charging toward the bottom of the field. As he scraped against the fence on the turn, Sooze leaned over to her right and managed to wrap her arms around a fence post. Stormy continued racing down the field at full speed, leaving his rider dangling. Sooze dropped to the ground, badly shaken but unharmed.

Mr. Chambers joined Sooze, steadying her shoulders before looking into her eyes. "Are you all right?"

"What on earth were you trying to do?" Mrs. Chambers puffed as she and Skye approached.

"That was dumb!" Skye panted. "You could've killed yourself!" Echoing in Skye's brain was the thought, *And who else pulled a stupid stunt like that on a horse not too long ago?*

"Stupid horse!" Sooze complained as she glared at Stormy, munching grass down near the pond with reins dangling. "It wasn't my fault. Something spooked him."

"Yeah, right," Skye retorted. "I think the spook was on his back."

For the rest of the afternoon at Keystone Stables, the mood was somber and tense. Sooze's disobedience put pleasure on the back burner, and the business of running a ranch took over. While Mr. Chambers cut hay on the lower fields, Mrs. Chambers and the girls blanched twenty dozen ears of corn, bagged them, and stored them in one of the basement freezers.

While Sooze sulked and complained about the work, Skye and Morgan tried to eat as much corn as they bagged, told stupid jokes, and determined to change Mrs. Chambers' disgruntled mood.

"Man, is Mrs. C. ticked!" Skye whispered to Sooze over a boiling pot of corn. "You are gonna get it. Big time!"

"Watch me!" was Sooze's smart reply.

The mood at supper was somewhat lighter, however. If they had been practicing to eat politely before the Queen of England, everyone would have passed with flying colors. Mr. Chambers reviewed the next week's activities, and Mrs. Chambers talked about a shopping trip, all with the utmost restraint. After supper, the family met in the living room for devotions and a family discussion.

"Just remember, girls," Mr. Chambers said as he glanced up from his Bible, you can't earn your way to heaven. In the Book of Ephesians it says that eternal life is a result of God's grace—his undeserved favor. It's a gift you can't see but you can receive by faith. All you need to do is believe that Jesus Christ died and rose again for your sins and ask him to forgive you."

Skye fixed her gaze on a vase of flowers on the end table beside Mr. Chambers.

"My life has never been the same since I did that many years ago," Mrs. Chambers added. "Girls, God gives you a peace in your heart that's hard to understand."

Morgan smiled and directed her words at Skye and Sooze. "I accepted Christ as my Savior after I moved in here, and it's so cool having the Lord as my best friend.

He's always there to help me through tough times. Now I finally have my head screwed on straight instead of making stupid choices that get me in trouble."

Skye stared at the floor and couldn't help but notice that Sooze was doing the same thing.

"The Lord does help us with our decisions, girls." Mr. Chambers laid down his Bible. "Eileen and I pray daily that we will lead you girls down the right cow path," he added in a show of returning humor. "Right now we need to discuss what happened earlier today with Stormy. Sooze, since you disobeyed in front of the whole family, everyone is included in this discussion. We value all of your opinions on decisions we must make. We want you to tell us how you see things."

"It wasn't my fault," Sooze snapped. "I told you I know how to ride."

"She has been to riding camps a couple of times, Mr. C.," Skye added in support.

"Skye," Mrs. Chambers leaned forward on the sofa, "you know our horses are not like camp horses and ponies. We've warned you all well in advance how much training it takes to handle one of these show horses. It's a big deal. We're talking about your safety, the horse's safety, and thousands of dollars."

Mr. Chambers now assumed a rigid pose in his chair with his elbows on the armrests, his hands folded in front of his mustache. "Sooze, I'm afraid you've broken the all-time record for the kid to get grounded the quickest after moving in. If it were a lesser offense, we might go a little easier. But we just cannot tolerate reckless behavior around the horses. Somebody could get killed."

"But I told you it wasn't my fault!" Sooze whined, slumping in her chair and crossing her ankles with a jolt.

You better cool it, Skye thought, *or they'll tack on another week for griping*. "Sooze—" Skye caught Sooze's eye and shook her head in silent warning.

Mr. Chambers spelled out the sentence. "Young lady, you will be grounded for two weeks. No mall, no trips, no recreation room, no phone. You will still be expected to do your household chores and yard work, but the barn and the horses are off limits. The rest of us will cover your chores down there.

"Skye and Morgan may still visit you in your room each night for a half hour, and you will still go with us to church. Other than that, life will be crawling a little slowly for you. Now, you don't have to lock yourself up in your room. You are not in jail. We want you at every meal and in all the family devotions and discussions. But your other activities will have to wait."

"That's so not fair!" Sooze griped. "You're not givin' me a chance. I hate this place!"

"Sooze," Morgan said, "why don't you give us a chance—and this place?"

"We love you and want you here with us," Mrs. Chambers said. "But you have to cooperate."

"All your rules are stupid," Sooze said. "My mother doesn't make me do nothin'. I can do whatever I want!"

"Did that make you happy, Sooze?" Mrs. Chambers asked.

"When I get what I want—which is most of the time," Sooze answered smartly.

"Can't you give her another chance?" Skye pleaded.

"Oh, but we are," Mr. Chambers reasoned. "She's getting the same chance as you and Morgan. We're trying to help you girls learn what's most important in life. Sooze, you'll get nowhere thinking everything that happens to you is someone else's fault. We're praying that you accept this discipline and learn from it. You may go to your room. Morgan and Skye may visit you later for a while if they'd like. And remember," he said, "we're doing this to help you, not to hurt you."

"Yeah, right," Sooze sassed.

Sooze hurried out of the room and ran down the hall. She slammed her bedroom door so hard, it shook the whole house.

Uh, oh. I smell big trouble, Skye thought.

Before bedtime, Skye knocked on Sooze's door with Morgan trailing right behind.

"Hey, what's up?" Skye asked, as she gently pushed open the door.

"Nothin'. Just go away and leave me alone!" Sooze fumed, her angry body leaning up against the head-board with her sneakers planted firmly on the bed. With elbows on her knees, she pressed her head with her hands. Obvious pain shrouded her face.

"No problem," Morgan said, pivoting and heading out the doorway. "I have better things to do than listen to this baloney. Later! Much later!"

"Another headache?" Skye asked as she turned toward the door. "No wonder you're in such a lousy mood. I'll see you in the morning."

"No—wait," Sooze whispered. "C'mere."

"I wish you'd make up your mind. What's up?" Skye asked as she sat on the edge of the bed.

Sooze ignored the question, sliding next to Skye, "I'm outta here tonight. Are you with me?"

"Are you crazy?" Skye whispered loudly. "Where would you go? And how? Sooze, think! This might land you in Chesterfield for good."

"Well, big deal!" Sooze growled. "What's the difference? They are not gonna tell me what to do—here—or anyplace else."

"Where are you going? And how?"

"Skye, sometimes you are as thick as that wall. The Chambers have a piece of junk with four wheels they call a truck. Right?"

"Yeah—so?"

"Well?" Sooze asked.

"Well what?"

"I'm taking that truck, and I'm history. I've watched every time Mr. C. has parked it, and he always throws the keys under the seat. So, are you comin' with me or not?"

Skye chewed her lip, biting back the fear in her heart. "Sooze, this is so not a good idea. You can't drive! You're only fourteen."

"Hey, been there, done that. There's nothin' to it," Sooze said smugly. "I'm only askin' you one more time. Are you comin' or not?"

"But where to? And for how long? Where will you stay? How will you eat?"

"I told you I have friends all over the place. Some of them live just an hour from here. They'll hide us until I can think this through. I don't need this goody two-shoes life."

"I—I don't know. It sounds really stupid to me."

"Fine," Sooze mocked. "If you never wanna see me again, that's fine. But if you wanna help me, meet me down at the truck at midnight."

Skye pulled the curtain back on her bedroom window. The clear night sky twinkled with a curtain of stars, and a full moon lit up everything outside with a soft white glow. She studied the backyard intently, focusing on a figure creeping her way down to the barn and slipping into the front seat of the old pickup. Skye lifted her window an inch and listened to the familiar sound of the engine grinding before turning over. With headlights out, the truck crawled along the dirt road from the side of the barn, past the house, and onto the main road. There it sat idling.

Sooze, you are so dead! Skye couldn't let her go like this. She inched her window up a couple of feet, slid out quietly, and darted across the lawn. Panting, she reached the road and ran around to the door on the passenger side of the truck. Carefully, she squeaked it open and slid in.

"So you're not so chicken after all," Sooze whispered. She pulled the knob for the lights, jammed the gearshift into drive, and the truck crept down the road away from Keystone Stables.

"Sooze, this is so not the way to do this," Skye said. "Maybe you can be placed in a different foster home if you hate it here so much."

"I am so sick of people telling me what to do!" Sooze's voice rose in anger as the truck's speed increased rapidly. "I have had it up to here with rules." She lifted her hand and made a slicing motion across her neck.

In an instant, with only one inexperienced hand on its steering wheel, the truck wavered. It jerked, and the tires caught on the asphalt berm of the narrow road, causing the truck to fishtail.

Skye's body jolted and banged against the door. As she landed, her eyes fixed on a fast approaching horseshoe turn.

"Look out!" Skye screamed in horror. "You're going too fast! Slow down!"

Sooze fought the wheel to steady the truck, now completely out of control.

"Oh, no!" Skye screamed. And then everything went black.

Chapter Five

Skye lay on a hospital bed with a gauze patch taped above one eyebrow. Scrapes and bruises covered her entire body. She ached as though she had been twisted into a pretzel and tied up for days.

What happened? Where am I? she wondered. Then it all came flooding back. Groaning, she finally managed to turn her head just enough to see a clock on a tan wall.

Three o'clock! It's been hours.

Time to think often found itself on the bottom of Skye's priority list. Thinking left her feeling depressed and alone, even in the middle of a cheering crowd at the Madison football games. But now, for the first time in her short, thirteen-year-old life, Skye allowed herself to consider what could have happened, and she felt terribly alone.

Oh God! Thank you for sending someone to help us. Skye gasped a sudden breath. *Did I just thank God for saving me? The God I have no time for? What if I'd died? Where would I be now? What if this had been my last day on Earth?*

Skye wondered. *What would I have to show God, so he would let me into heaven?*

"Nothing," Skye whispered out loud. "Nothing but a rotten attitude and a court record as long as my arm."

A flood of tears drenched her cheeks, and an overwhelming sense of guilt flooded her soul.

God would never want me! she thought. *I'm too rotten!*

Then it was as if Mr. Chambers was standing right beside her. She remembered what he'd said to them: "You can't earn your way to heaven. It's God's gift. Just ask him to forgive you of your sins, and you'll be a new person, inside and out!"

Then Skye remembered Morgan's words: "Jesus is the best friend I have. He's always there when I need him."

I need you right now, God! Skye's heart cried out.

Just then, a pretty nurse with dark hair and kind eyes came through the doors. "So we're awake, are we?" she said. "As soon as the doctor checks you out, there are some people who are anxious to see you."

Again, the doors opened, and a man in a white lab coat, with straight black hair, hurried in. Reading glasses were perched on his nose as he glanced at a clipboard.

"Skye Nicholson," he said, flipping through some papers. "I'm Doctor Wang. You are one fortunate young lady. You and your friend both hit your heads on the windshield. Someone's been watching out for you it seems," he said as he carefully examined Skye's head, neck, and shoulders.

The doctor nodded at the nurse, who walked to the door and waved. As if on cue, Mrs. Chambers rushed into the room with her husband following close behind.

"Honey, are you all right?" Mrs. Chambers asked.

"You sure know how to scare the wits out of us," Mr. Chambers said, forcing a smile. "What were you two trying to do?"

"Where's Sooze? Is she okay?" Skye rubbed her swollen, tear-soaked eyes.

"Sooze is in another room," Mr. Chambers said. "She's got a nasty bump on her head. She's still a little dizzy, but the doctor thinks she'll be okay. It's a miracle you two weren't seriously injured—or killed! The truck is totaled, but God had his hand of protection on you two. No doubt about it."

"When will she be released?" Mrs. Chambers asked.

"We need to keep her for observation. You can probably take her home tomorrow. However," Dr. Wang directed his words back to Skye, "you take it easy for a few days. You've got some serious bruising, and those stitches above your eye need time to heal. No cartwheels or jumping out of airplanes or anything. Okay?"

"What about Sooze—Sue Bodmer—across the hall?" Mrs. Chambers asked. "May we take her with us, too?"

Dr. Wang looked through another set of papers. "Hmm," he said, deep in thought. "Preliminary skull X-rays show something that we'd like to examine a little further. She got a nasty bump on the left side of her head.

We'd like to keep her a few more days for observation and run more tests. It's probably nothing, but we want to make sure. She's complaining of a severe headache."

"Sooze has a lot of headaches," Skye said.

Mrs. Chambers' face reflected deep concern. "She's been our foster child for less than a week. She hasn't told us about the headaches, and her health records show no such problem."

"Like I said," Dr. Wang replied, "it's probably nothing, but I would like our neurosurgeon to take a look at the test results. We're going to move her upstairs now. If you wait a little longer, you should be able to see her."

"Yes, we'll wait," Mr. Chambers said. "We'll go grab a quick cup of coffee and wait in Skye's room."

"The nurse will let you know when you can see Susan," Dr. Wang said. "She'll direct you to Susan's room. I'm sure she'll be very glad to see you."

In the dimly-lit hospital room, Skye sipped chocolate milk from a carton while Mr. and Mrs. Chambers drank coffee from Styrofoam cups like two robots. All three struggled with heavy eyelids.

Mrs. Chambers broke the hush. "This place makes you want to whisper, doesn't it?"

"Yeah," Mr. Chambers said. Finishing his coffee, he stared at Skye. "How do you feel?"

"Okay," she said. "Just a little stiff is all."

Mrs. Chambers sipped her coffee. "Where did you girls think you were going at that hour? And what made you two think Sooze could drive a truck?"

"You know Sooze," Skye answered. "She thinks she can do anything. I sure hope she's all right."

"We do too," Mrs. Chambers said. "Tom, you did call her mother, didn't you?"

"Yes," he answered. "She said she'd check on Sooze in the morning. I guess she's been through this kind of thing with her daughter so many times, she thinks Sooze is invincible."

"Skye," Mrs. Chambers said, "do you realize you could have been killed tonight? What were you thinking?"

Skye placed her empty carton on her tray table. "You probably won't believe me, but I was trying to stop her. She wanted to drive to some friend's house about an hour from here. I went with her to try to talk her out of it. I know I could've been killed!"

Skye felt her face flush hot. Tears streamed down her face and onto her hospital gown.

"What's the matter, honey?" Mrs. Chambers gently rubbed Skye's back and handed her a tissue.

"I'm just so sorry," was all Skye could manage between sobs.

"We know you are," Mr. Chambers said. "There will be some consequences later, but for now we want you to know that we still love you."

"I don't mean just this," Skye said, rubbing her tear-filled eyes. "I mean I'm sorry for everything. Mr. C., I've been thinking about what you said in devotions the other night—you know, about God's gift? I want to ask Jesus to forgive me and save me. Would I have to wait until church on Sunday to do that?"

Mr. Chambers' mustache twitched as his face broke into a smile. "Skye, that's the best news ever. We've been praying every day that you would feel the need to turn your life over to God. And—no—you don't need to wait until Sunday. You can do it right here—right now."

"What do I do?" Skye asked.

Mrs. Chambers reached over and took Skye's hand.

"We can pray together right here," Mr. Chambers responded. "Remember what we've said about God being so holy that sin can't exist in his presence? As a righteous judge, the sentence he requires for sin and rebellion is death. But as soon as the sentence was announced, God asked his own Son, Jesus Christ, to die on the cross in your place. And that's exactly what he did. That's the grace I was talking about. Jesus wasn't guilty of anything, but he took all the sin of the world, including everything you've ever done wrong, and died for you so that you wouldn't have to."

Skye couldn't believe what she was hearing. "You mean, I should have gotten the death penalty, but Jesus took it for me? I don't understand. Why would he do that?"

"He did that because he loves you, Skye, more than you will ever fully know. Tell you what," Mr. Chambers said, placing his cup aside, "let's pray right now. God doesn't expect any fancy words, Skye. All he wants to know is that you want to accept his wonderful gift and receive forgiveness."

Folding her hands, Skye bowed her head. Different from all the other times she had prayed, she closed her eyes, concentrating on Jesus, the one who had always loved her in spite of her faults.

"Dear God," she said, "I know I've been rotten, and I don't blame you if you're mad at me. But if it's true that you want to forgive me, I'm asking you to do that right now. I'm sorry for everything I've ever done wrong. Jesus, thank you for taking my sin on yourself, so I can be forgiven and go to heaven. Amen."

Skye glanced at the only two people who had ever shown real care and concern for her. She couldn't contain her smile as she reflected on what she had just done.

"Skye," Mrs. Chambers said, eyes sparkling with joy, "we love you so much."

"Yes, we do," Mr. Chambers added, "and according to the Bible, God does too. Now, young lady, you are part of another family—the family of God."

A deep breath of air filled Skye's lungs, reminding her of the bruises that made it painful to breathe. But it didn't matter how she felt on the outside because, for the first time in her life, Skye felt really clean on the inside. At last, she was free from the anger and hatred that had weighed her down. Now she was free to love, starting with the two greatest people she had ever known.

"And I love you both—Mom and Dad."

Chapter Six

At home, Skye focused on her nightstand clock and shot upright in bed. Pain flashed through her whole body, even though one whole day had passed since the accident.

"Ten o'clock! Ow! Oh—oh," she groaned and fell back on her pillow. Then she remembered. The accident—the hospital—the cut above her eye—the bruises. No wonder she felt like she'd been run over by a truck!

Skye struggled to roll over and sit on the edge of her bed and then caught a glimpse of herself in the dresser mirror. *Yikes!* she thought.

Skye unfolded herself, one sore limb at a time, and struggled to stand. *It's cool that the Chambers let me sleep in. I wonder how Sooze is doing?*

Despite the bruises on the outside, Skye felt as though a cool stream flowed through her soul, bringing peace. Now she could face the morning with a smile, one that came from the depths of her new spirit. She couldn't get over how different she felt—new. She limped to her window and looked out.

The day was already a muggy, overcast gray, but even the weather couldn't dampen the sunshine Skye felt inside. Something special *had* happened! Like a dirty stable made clean, her own heart had been "mucked out." This was the second day of her new, sparkling-clean life with God. The Chambers had kept her in bed and quiet after she got home from the hospital the day before, but today she would be able to talk to Morgan. She could hardly wait to tell her the good news.

Despite her pain, Skye hurried to dress and brush her hair, still long, healthy, and shining. She hobbled out of her bedroom and made her way down the hallway into the dining room. The welcoming fragrance of coffee and buttered toast greeted her along with Mr. and Mrs. Chambers.

The couple sat close to one another, enjoying a late breakfast. The Westies, Tip and Ty, crouched under the table, stalking any handouts that might come their way.

"Did Mary Brannigan call you?" Mrs. Chambers asked her husband. "Her computer froze, and she thinks her hard drive crashed. I saw her at the market yesterday."

"No, not yet. I hope she does though. I can always use the business." Mr. Chambers then directed his attention to Skye. "Well, good morning, and where do you think you're going?"

Mrs. Chambers swallowed a bite of toast. "Honey, you can't possibly do chores today. We're going to do them for you. Oh my, just look at your poor sweet face!"

"Where's Morgan?" Skye said as she leaned against the table. "You didn't tell her, did you? Where is she?"

"Whoa, take it easy, girl. She's down at the barn," Mr. Chambers said, forking the last of his scrambled eggs.

"And yes, we told her about the accident," Mrs. Chambers added, sipping her coffee.

"No, no, I don't mean about the accident. I mean about me—and God—what I did at the hospital."

"No, we didn't tell her," Mrs. Chambers said. "We figured you'd want to tell her all about that yourself. Now sit down and have some breakfast."

"But I wanna tell her right now. Can I? Please? Then I'll eat."

"Sure," Mr. Chambers grinned. "The decision you made to accept Christ was the most important one you'll ever make. Go on."

Mrs. Chambers smiled. "I'll put the eggs on 'warm' in the microwave. Now go ahead before you forget what happened." Both she and Mr. Chambers laughed.

Skye hobbled down to the barn as fast as her aching legs would go. She squeezed through the sliding door and hurried past every stall. Frustrated, she finally yelled, "Morgan!"

"In the tack room!" Morgan yelled back.

Skye hurried to the small room decked with saddles mounted on wooden struts and bridles hanging on wall hooks. The pungent aromas of leather, horses, and hay saturated the cool barn air. Morgan sat in the center of the room, polishing a saddle mounted on a sawhorse.

"Hey, sleepyhead! You're finally among the land of the living!" Morgan kidded and then looked up. Her green eyes gawked in disbelief. "No way! Look at those black eyes! What were you two trying to prove?"

Skye limped to the center of the room. Overturning an old bucket, she arranged her aching body gingerly in front of Morgan who went back to soaping the saddle.

"You know the fair is only a month away," Morgan started. "We have tons of work to do before—"

"Morgan, I've gotta tell you somethin'," Skye interrupted.

"If it's about the accident and Sooze, I already know. Mr. and Mrs. C. told me. I sure hope her test results come out okay. She may get shipped out after pulling that little stunt. Man, that was stupid. And you too! Where's your head, girl?"

"No, I don't mean about Sooze. It's about me."

Morgan paused, her freckled face troubled. "*You're* not leaving, are you?"

"No, it's nothin' like that. I did somethin' last night that I had never done before. In fact, I thought I would *never* do it."

"Now what? Did you get yourself into more hot water?"

"Will you be quiet for a minute and listen?" Skye demanded.

Morgan snapped her head up and blinked with surprise. "All right! What?"

"Well, that truck accident made me think things through. All that stuff you and the Chambers have been telling me about God and all—well—all of a sudden, it sank in. I mean about needing God in my life, just like you said, and—well—last night at the hospital I asked Jesus Christ to forgive me and to come into my life. I can't believe it, Morgan, but I feel like a whole new person. Like you've been telling me, it is *so* cool."

Nothing came out of Morgan's open mouth, and her eyes grew wide as though Skye had grown a second head.

"You're kidding!" Morgan finally screeched. She dropped the cream tin and cloth in her lap and reached her arms toward Skye. "That is *so* great!"

"Ow!" Skye said when the two embraced. She pulled away sharply. "I am one big bruise."

"Sorry," Morgan said, "but that is such great news! Wait till Pastor Newman and the kids at church hear this. They've all been praying for you, you know. Even Chad."

"Chad?" Skye felt her face flush.

"Yeah, you heard me. The one and only Chad Dressler," Morgan giggled. "You know, he really likes you. I mean—he really, *really* likes you. Wait till he hears that you've become a Christian. He'll be totally impressed. And wait till he gets a look at the new you!"

"Very funny!" Skye hurled back. Then her tone softened. "I like him too—sort of."

"Sort of?" Morgan cackled as she picked up the saddle cream and cloth. "Sort of? Yeah, right. Every time his name is mentioned you turn five shades of red. I think you've got a crush on him. Anyway, I'm so glad you've become a Christian. Now I can call you my sister for real—my sister in Christ."

For once Skye was glad it rained in Shade Valley the next three days. Watching Morgan ride would have been pure agony, but Skye's battered body wouldn't have been able to even sit on Champ. By the end of the week, the rain stopped. Feeling well enough to ride, Skye joined Morgan for a quick breakfast and headed to the barn. While low threatening clouds hid the blast of the summer sun, they worked their horses in the large paddock, practicing for the upcoming horse show at the Snyder County Fair.

Morgan had just finished working Blaze in barrel racing and now sat on her mount, watching Skye practice for the Advanced Trail Class. Skye, in the center of the field, was engrossed in maneuvering Champ through a wooden gate stationed between two posts.

"Careful, Skye," Morgan cautioned. "Champ tends to swing his rump too far to the left when you reach for the gate. If he bumps that post, you'll get docked some points!"

"Got it," Skye replied. "I'll try it again, this time a little slower." Skye positioned the horse carefully and reached down, gently swinging open the gate.

"Easy, Champ," she said. She rubbed his belly with her left leg at the same time she tugged his reins to the right, prompting him to step sideways. Carefully, she nudged him through the narrow opening and turned him around. She reached down for the gate and clicked it closed while her horse stood like a Civil War statue.

"Voilà!" Morgan cheered. "That one was too perfect! Too bad you can't videotape it and send it to the judges. You'd take first place!"

Skye laughed as she jogged Champ toward Morgan. "He'll do it again," Skye insisted as she reached down and stroked the horse's silky mane. "This wasn't the first time. And he's been great with the water obstacle and the log step-over. I just need to catch up with his brilliance!"

"How's it going, girls?" a man's voice yelled from the backyard.

Skye turned to see Mr. Chambers walking toward them from the house. "Great, Mr. C.—uh—I mean Dad," Skye yelled back. "Wanna see Champ do the gate thing?"

"And Blaze is still blazing up a storm in her barrel cuts, Mr. C. You wanna see a run of that too?" Morgan asked.

"I've got some work to do first," Mr. Chambers said, leaning up against the fence. "Maybe later in the afternoon when I get done."

"Did you bring Sooze home?" Skye asked.

"Yes, we did." Mr. Chambers' face grew deadly serious.

"Well, how is she? Does she get to stay here?" Morgan asked.

"Yeah," Skye added, "and *where* is she?"

"Skye, she wants to see you—alone," her foster dad said as he gestured toward the picnic grove in a clump of trees next to the house. "You go ahead, and I'll cool down Champ."

"What's the matter?" Skye asked as she dismounted. "Does she have to leave? Is she okay? What's going on?"

Sensitive to the situation, Morgan prodded Blaze and they started walking away. "I'll wait for you over at the barn, Mr. C."

Mr. Chambers crawled between the boards of the fence and took Champ's reins. "Sooze wants to tell you herself. Now go on," he gestured again, "she's waiting."

Beyond the fence, Skye could see the picnic grove with towering pines swaying in a strong breeze offset by low threatening clouds. A lone figure, her back toward the field, stood silhouetted by the pavilion and thick woods.

"Sooze!" Skye tried to yell. She squeezed through the fence boards and pushed her body as fast as it would go across the lawn, over the bridge at the stream, and to the pavilion. By the time she got there, Skye was gasping for breath, her nostrils filled with the heavy, moist scent of pine.

I hope Sooze isn't in terrible trouble, she thought anxiously. *We* never *should've taken that truck!*

"Sooze!" Skye gasped a quick breath. "What's going on? Do you have to leave?"

Chapter Seven

Slowly Sooze turned, her bruised face flooded with tears. Her body, covered with black and blue scrapes and bruises, was a carbon copy of Skye's.

"They did a whole bunch of tests." Sooze's voice sounded strangled. "I've got a brain tumor—and I'm scared."

"A—what?" was all Skye could say. Disbelief threaded its way through every inch of her aching body.

"A tumor. They found this thing in my head. That's what gives me the terrible headaches."

Sooze sat down at the table, dropped her head onto her arms, and began to sob. Still standing, Skye felt paralyzed by what she had just heard.

Sooze has a brain tumor? Skye's thoughts were racing.

Skye found herself groping for the right words to say— any words to say.

"Just be a friend in the tough times," Pastor Newman's words from one of his sermons prodded Skye's memory.

"Jesus is your best friend, and he's always there. You, too, can be that kind of friend to someone in need." Skye lowered herself gently and slipped an arm around Sooze.

As though God were weeping too, the skies opened and raindrops pelted the shingled roof, dripping on the carpet of pine around the pavilion. With a refreshing wave of summer rain, the air immediately grew cooler. Skye took a shaky deep breath, her nostrils now filled with an even more pungent scent of pine. In seconds, a steady downpour brought a distant roll of thunder, and ribbons of water cascaded from the roof into tiny furrows around the pavilion's cement slab.

Sooze raised her head and wiped her eyes with her fists. "What am I gonna do, Skye?"

Skye squeezed Sooze's shoulder. "I don't know," she answered. "But I do know someone who can show you what to do."

"Who?" Sooze's voice filled with hope. She turned and looked at Skye.

"God," Skye said.

Sooze's eyes, bloodshot and troubled, searched Skye's. "What?"

"I said God can help you."

Sooze slid away from Skye and gave her a nasty scowl. "Where are you comin' from with this God stuff again? I told you the other day I didn't wanna hear it, and now I double mean it! If God is so great, why would he let this happen to me?"

"I don't know—"

"Well—when you've got some answers, let me know," Sooze cried. "I'm the one with this thing growin' in my head! I don't need anyone shoving religion down my throat along with everything else. Got it?"

"Got it," Skye said sadly. "But I want you to know that I'm here for you—and God is too."

Skye studied the puffballs of white floating in the brilliant blue sky that had come after the afternoon rain. She sucked in a lungful of cool evening air as she stood with Mrs. Chambers on the lopsided front porch of Sooze's house, waiting.

"Well, ain't you a sight for sore eyes! Look at them bruises." Skye could hear Mrs. Bodmer even over the television chatter inside the house.

"Thanks for caring!" Skye heard Sooze snapping back.

A few seconds passed until Sooze said glumly from the doorway, "Mom says it's okay to come in."

Skye followed Sooze and Mrs. Chambers into a living room stacked with boxes and newspapers. Mrs. Bodmer lay on a haggard brown sofa that looked like a haunted-house movie prop. Her pudgy body, dressed in a cherry-red halter top and jean shorts, absorbed the breeze from her favorite fan, now resting on a coffee table. The bottled-blonde, frizzy hair framing her face swirled in the breeze. Her stubby, ring-clad fingers, now decorated with long purple fingernails, latched onto a beer can in one hand and a cigarette in the other.

"Come on in," Mrs. Bodmer's gruff voice ordered above the noisy TV, "and shut the door tight. We don't need any more flies in here!"

Skye pulled a tattered screen door closed, her eyes searching for flies.

"It's good to see you again," Mrs. Chambers said loudly above the noisy TV. Sooze flopped into a sagging green chair and closed her eyes. Her head rested back on the dirty upholstery.

Mrs. Chambers continued, trying to be heard, "We need to talk to you about your daughter, Mrs. Bodmer! About her progress so far—and—well—her health!"

Mrs. Bodmer clicked the TV off, sucked greedily on her cigarette, and exhaled a stream of smoke from her nose. The fan blew it wildly into the musty air. Folding her arms, she squinted through the last puff of smoke that blew back in her face.

"Yeah, how's the kid doin'? When I called the hospital this morning, they said she was sleeping, so I didn't want them to wake her. So what's goin' on?" She looked at Sooze with obvious suspicion. "You ain't gettin' into more trouble, are you, Susan? From the looks of you, trouble should've been your middle name!"

A heavy silence hung over the green chair.

"Skye, why don't you and Sooze find something to do, so Mrs. Bodmer and I can talk alone."

"Sure," said Skye. Sooze reluctantly pulled herself out of the green chair, and the girls disappeared up the stairs to Sooze's old room.

Mrs. Chambers shifted her solid frame from one foot to the other and then took a seat in the chair Sooze had vacated.

"Mrs. Bodmer, I have some troubling news. The doctors ran some tests on Susan while she was at the hospital."

"Tests?" Mrs. Bodmer said. She took a gulp from her can.

"Yes," Mrs. Chambers said. "We had a meeting with two different doctors earlier today, and they think Sooze has a brain tumor."

"A brain tumor?" Slowly, Mrs. Bodmer forced her body forward onto the edge of the sofa, set her can on the coffee table, and eyed Mrs. Chambers skeptically. "That's ridiculous!" she snorted. "What are you people trying to pull?"

"I assure you, it's true," Mrs. Chambers answered. "I know this is a shock."

"Now wait a minute. You're telling me my kid has a brain tumor? Does that mean an operation?" Mrs. Bodmer asked.

"No. Surgery isn't an option because of the location of the tumor. Next week the doctors want to run another series of tests, and if the results are the same, Sooze will need to begin chemotherapy and then radiation. The doctors would like you to come in with us at that time, so they can go over the test results with all of us."

"Well, how much is that gonna cost me?" Mrs. Bodmer scowled. "I don't got no insurance, you know. And how do they know it's a brain tumor anyway? It could be a mistake."

"That's the reason for running a second series of tests," Mrs. Chambers said, "just to be sure. Mrs. Bodmer, I hope you realize that this is serious. Hopefully, with the treatments, she'll be okay. The tumor is what's been giving her the headaches. And the costs will be covered by the state since Sooze is in foster care."

Mrs. Bodmer stared at Mrs. Chambers. Then she returned to her original position on the sofa and took a long drink from the beer can. "Susan ain't gonna die, is she?"

"I hope not," Mrs. Chambers answered. "We're praying for her."

At the mention of prayer, Mrs. Bodmer sniffed loudly. "Yeah, right," she huffed sarcastically. "God's done so much for us in the past."

"Mrs. Bodmer," Mrs. C. continued, "the doctors are very hopeful that the treatments will curb the growth of the tumor. We're all hoping they have found it in time. Sooze knows about all of this. She sensed that something was wrong and pressed us to tell her. It's an awfully big deal for a kid her age. She really needs all the support we can give her right now."

Sooze and Skye reappeared on the stairs and then slowly made their way back over to where the women were sitting. Mrs. Bodmer stared intently at her daughter and then took one last puff on her cigarette before squashing out the stub.

"Now wait!" She shook her head and drew her hands through her frizzy hair, flattening it against her head before it went back to its dance with the fan. "This is all goin' too fast." She studied Sooze again. "You mean my kid's *so* sick that she needs radiation and chemo?"

"Sooze, I've told your mother what's going on with you."

Mrs. Bodmer looked Sooze up and down one more time. "Susan, this ain't one of your dirty tricks again, is it?" Mrs. Bodmer growled. "If it is, it ain't one bit funny."

"I assure you it isn't," Mrs. Chambers said. "Sooze didn't cause this. It just happened."

"Don't worry, Mumsy," Sooze said sarcastically. "It's going to be loads of fun. First, I'll lose my hair, and then, I'll be throwing up my guts. Who knows—maybe I'll even die. That would be a lucky break for you, wouldn't it?"

Mrs. Bodmer reached for her cigarettes and lighter. She drew a cigarette from the pack, turned the fan off, and lit up. Sucking in a long breath, she then exhaled and filled the room with putrid clouds of gray.

"Well, ain't life grand!" she hissed. "Like I don't got enough trouble. Now I got a sick kid."

"Before we leave," Mrs. Chambers said, "we'd like to pray with you and Sooze. Prayer always helps in times like these when we don't know which way to turn."

Mrs. Bodmer took a drink from her can and then scowled.

"No thank you!" she harped. "I ain't never had no need for God, and I don't need him now. You can just take your prayers and be on your merry way. No god would let this stuff happen to me."

"I'm sorry you feel that way," Mrs. Chambers said. "God has helped me through some pretty tough times. He—"

"I said no!" Mrs. Bodmer shouted. "Like I said, you can just get on down the road!" Then she looked at Sooze. "And you let me know what's goin' on, okay?"

Sooze rolled her eyes and, without as much as a glance at her mother, headed out the front door, letting the screen door slam behind her. Without a word, Skye started toward the door.

Mrs. Chambers turned to leave, still looking at Mrs. Bodmer. "Let us know if you can go with us next week. It would be good for you to hear this directly from the doctors. And, of course, you're always welcome to come out to Keystone Stables for a visit. I'm sure Sooze would appreciate that."

Mrs. Bodmer clicked on the TV with the remote control. Again sitcom laughter blasted through the room.

"Yeah, thanks," she slurred, settling into her nest. "Call me."

"We certainly will," Mrs. Chambers said. "We certainly will."

Chapter Eight

Skye, look at this cool game I'm playing on the Internet." Morgan worked the computer keyboard like a secretary back from vacation. "It's called Asteroids."

The walls of the Chambers' game room vibrated with the noise of electronic laser blasts.

"Yeah, I've done that at the mall zillions of times." Skye shouted above the noise of her own game of Nintendo. "One time I scored thirty thousand before I got zapped."

"I wonder how Sooze is." Morgan said.

"I don't think she feels too hot, especially since her first treatment. Man, did she throw up after that! And her poor hair! She looks like a scarecrow with a bad hair day."

"I hope the doctor has a good report. It's been two weeks since the chemo."

Skye glanced at a wall clock above her computer. "She and Mom oughta be back soon. We could all use some good news. I've never known anybody before who had a brain tumor. Kind of scary, isn't it?"

"Yeah. But I know God could help Sooze if she'd just let him. It has to be scary without having him on your team.

"Yikes! Get over there!" Morgan said to the screen.

The outside entrance door to their right opened, the girls oblivious to it.

"Hey, what's happening?" Mrs. Chambers spoke above the game racket as she walked up behind Skye. "Hard at work helping Tom paint the fence, I see," she teased.

"Oh, we're gonna help him in just a minute," Skye said, "as soon as these last games are done. Where's Sooze?"

"She'll be down in a minute," Mrs. Chambers answered. "She wanted to do something first. By the way, girls, I have sandwiches in the fridge down here if you want to eat before you attack the paint can."

Skye's game came to a crashing halt. She shut it down and followed Mrs. Chambers to the kitchenette.

"Mom, what did the doctor say about Sooze?"

Mrs. Chambers opened the refrigerator and pulled out a covered plate of sandwiches and a plastic pitcher of iced tea. "Well, the oncologist is quite hopeful that we caught this thing in time. He plans to give Sooze three more chemo treatments followed by radiation. That's supposed to shrink the tumor or kill it all together. They're pretty optimistic. I just wish Sooze's mother would join the process."

Morgan came in at the tail end of the discussion. "How often will she get those treatments?"

"Once a month," Mrs. Chambers answered, handing wet wipes to the girls. "That's all a body can handle."

"Yeah," Skye said, pulling paper plates from a cupboard, "but it doesn't seem to be working with Sooze. She threw up her guts, and her hair's falling out in gobs." Skye ran a hand through her dark hair, pulling a lock forward to study a few strands. "That would freak me out—I don't think I could handle that."

"Yeah, no hair would be awful," Morgan agreed.

"Girls, when your life's at stake, you look at things in a whole different light," Mrs. C. said. "Which would you choose? Your hair or your life? Getting sick and losing your hair is part of the process, unfortunately. Sooze needs our prayers and support right now. Just encourage her as much as you can. She needs some good friends right now." She poured iced tea into three paper cups on the counter and smiled. "Let's pray over this feast, and we'll dig in."

Skye bowed her head and prayed: "Dear God, please help Sooze to feel better and get well, and thank you for this food. Bless it in Jesus' name. Amen."

"Hey, guys," Sooze's tired voice said.

Skye turned toward the doorway, her glance falling on a girl who had lost considerable weight, whose skin was pallid, and whose eyes seemed sunken more deeply into her thin face. But something was very different.

"Sooze," Skye exclaimed. "You have hair! Where—how—when?"

"Wow!" Morgan added. "That is too, too much! How did you get hair that fast? It's got to be a wig. Right?"

"Morgan, sometimes your brilliance knocks me out," Sooze slurred as she slowly squared the cowboy hat on her wig. "They told me at the hospital that you guys wouldn't even notice the difference from my real hair."

"It's true," Mrs. Chambers said.

Skye took a gulp of tea. "It looks so much like the real thing, the kids at church won't even notice. Too cool!"

"Would you like a ham sandwich, Sooze?" Mrs. C. said. We're having an early lunch, so these members of Fence Painters Anonymous can show their faces out in the paddock and help the poor man covered in paint out there."

"No, I'm not hungry," Sooze forced out, "just tired."

"Why don't you go lie down for a while," Mrs. Chambers suggested. "I'll wake you when we're ready to go to Maranatha. How does that sound?"

"I've got nothing better to do," Sooze complained. "Of course, I could go throw up for a while. Oh, sorry. I forgot you were eating."

"No problem." Skye went on eating her sandwich.

Mrs. C. smiled sympathetically. "Sooze, tell you what I'd like to do—that's if—and a big *if*—you feel better tomorrow. I've been thinking a lot about you and your horse situation. Maybe Stormy isn't the horse for you after all. I know the doctor wants you to take it real easy and not exert yourself. We'll be helping you with your chores. As far as riding is concerned—"

Sooze's eyes looked like they were ready to jump out of her head. "Don't tell me I can't ride the horses!"

Skye swallowed quickly and said, "Sooze, take it easy, but Mom's right. Maybe she would let you ride if you started with a smaller horse that's trained in a completely different way. Pepsi might be just right for you, right Mom?"

"Yes. That sounds like a good solution," Mrs. C. smiled.

"She's a beautiful, blood bay mare trained in Western only," Skye went on, "and she's a super trail horse with a lazy walk and easy gait. She'd never run off with you. Of course, you'd have to take it easy too. No horse enjoys a kick in the ribs. It's a wonder Stormy didn't buck you off the other day!"

"What does 'blood bay' mean?" Sooze asked.

"It means Pepsi is dark red brown," Morgan said.

"Like a Pepsi Cola with a shot of cherry," Skye added. "The 'bay' part means that she has a black mane and tail. Oh, and guess what? Pepsi is Champ's mommy. Right, Mrs. C?"

"Right. They both come from a long line of champion Quarter Horses. And, like I was saying, if you feel better tomorrow, we'll start riding lessons again, this time with Pepsi and, hopefully, a new attitude. What do you say?"

Sooze smiled weakly. "Great," she managed to say and raised her thumbs slowly.

Mrs. Chambers cleared the counter. "Okay, that's what we'll do. By the way, if you decide you want to eat later, just help yourself. There's iced tea here too. Now why don't you try to get some rest?"

"Sounds like a plan." Sooze's eyes managed a hopeful twinkle. "See you guys later."

A few days later, on a beautiful August afternoon, Skye and Sooze rode their horses through the woods. Ahead of the girls, Tippy and Tyler ran wildly, making frequent stops, sniffing every tree and rock they could find.

"Sooze, I think you'll do great in that Beginner's Showmanship Class at the horse show," Skye said, trying to be reassuring. "That thing in your head has slowed you down just enough to make you a greenhorn with an ounce or two of horse sense. After only a few weeks, you act like you've been hanging with horses all your life."

"I guess this brain tumor did do *one* good thing," Sooze said, tapping her hard hat. "No more kicking horses. Now it takes all my energy just to crawl on and click my tongue to say go." She reached down and stroked the coarse black mane on Pepsi's nodding head. "I'm trying not to show it, but I'm kinda freaking out over this horse show. You really think I can do it? What if I goof up? What if I'm even too tired to stand?"

"Just relax, will ya? Remember, you won't even be riding Pepsi. All you have to do is lead her around the show corral, square her up, and then blend into the sawdust. The judge will be looking at the horse, not you. Your most important part is getting her ready *before* the show. Brushing and oiling, polishing hooves, grooming her mane and tail. If you do a good job, Pepsi will be the star of the show. With a horse that's built like her, you could come home next week with a ribbon to match your Stetson. Besides, I'll help you."

The sound of squeaking saddles and clanking bridles accompanied the girls out from under a canopy of trees into a sun-drenched field. Skye loved the meadow, with its wildflowers, tall grasses, and the scent of scrub pines. They rode toward a campsite nestled at the base of three rolling hills in the distance, while the dogs leaped in the grass like dolphins.

They finally dismounted at the campsite, near a chuck wagon resting in a cluster of pines. To the wagon's left, nestled against a hill, stood an outdoor chapel with rows of hewn-out logs for pews. In the center of the chapel, a stone cross stood tall on a pile of mountain stone.

The altar, Skye thought. *That's where I found out what real love is all about.*

"Wow! This place is awesome!" Sooze exclaimed.

"This is Piney Hollow," Skye said. "The Chambers use it for picnics, church gatherings, and youth retreats."

"Youth retreats?"

"Yeah, kind of like camping or cookouts with the Youth for Truth club from church. Hey, I just remembered!" Skye's voice bubbled with excitement. "There's gonna be a retreat here in the fall with the church kids. It goes from Friday night till Saturday afternoon. The girls sleep in the loft of the barn, and the boys do their macho thing out here in tents and sleeping bags. All the kids will be here—Morgan, Robin, Melissa, Doug, Chad." Skye's face flushed, thinking about Chad. "Remember? You met them all at church."

"Yeah." Sooze scanned the area like a lost child looking for her mother. "But what do you do out here for two days? Watch the grass grow?"

The girls tied their horses to a hitching post and hung their hard hats on the saddle horns. They walked around the campfire area before Skye answered.

"Well, all the chow, including breakfast, will be cooked over a fire right here. Have you ever had eggs and bacon fried like that?" Skye asked.

"My mom and I never exactly went camping."

"It's *so* great! Mom even makes biscuits over the campfire. After we inhale breakfast, we usually go hiking and, of course, we have horses for trail riding. We spend a lot of time sitting around the campfire here and singing camp songs and choruses. Chad brought his guitar the last time, and Bobby brought his harmonica. Pastor Newman comes for supper on Friday. Then he talks to us at the chapel area." Skye plopped down on a stump and grabbed a stick to poke at a pile of ashes in the center of the fire circle. "Probably the first thing we'll do on Friday is go on a hayride."

Behind her, Sooze found a wooden crate and pulled it up next to Skye. "No way! You mean—that's it? Except for the horses, that sounds totally *boring*. Camp songs and choruses? Why can't we play our CDs and have some real fun?" She pretended to drink from a bottle.

"Get off it, Sooze," Skye answered. She ran both hands through her hair, moist with summer sweat. "You know the Chambers don't allow that kind of stuff. And, like, we're gonna have booze at a church outing?"

"You never know. After all, I'll be there," she smiled devilishly. "In fact," she added while reaching into her jeans pocket and pulling out a handful of pills, "look what I have now."

"Where'd you get those?" Skye asked with alarm.

"What, you think they wouldn't give me something to kill the pain?" She took four tablets from her hand and popped them into her mouth. "Want some?"

"Sooze, you can overdose on that stuff. What are you trying to do—finish yourself off?"

"Hey, get off my back. Right now it's the *only* way I'm gonna get through this. And you better not snitch."

"Like Mrs. C. isn't going to notice how fast they disappear."

"I'll just tell her my head felt like it was exploding. Man, I'm dyin' of thirst."

Skye rolled her eyes. "Yeah, it's a real scorcher today," she said in a feeble attempt to change the subject. "We should've brought canteens."

"Yeah, filled with something stronger than water!" Sooze's coarse laughter grated on Skye in the peaceful surroundings. "We could have a real party!"

Chapter Nine

The excitement of the week long Snyder County Fair ran through Skye's veins like electricity in a string of party lights—fun rides, pizza, and carnival games in perfect weather. But nothing made her heart pump as fast as the sights and smells of the horse show held every afternoon. For months, she and Champ had practiced for the Advanced Trail Class.

Skye's class finished, and the gate opened, allowing her and the rest of the field to exit the show ring. With her glowing smile, she maneuvered Champ around the perimeter of the corral past dozens of lined-up horse trailers. The Chambers, Morgan and Blaze, and Sooze with Pepsi had all clustered along the show ring fence, waiting for Skye to join them.

Skye's hair, drawn back into a tight bun, rested securely under a suede cowboy hat, complete with hawk feather and leather braid, leveled on her head to her eyebrows. Her leather-fringed vest over a checkered shirt had the number "65" pinned on the back. Her blue necktie, cowhide gloves, and polished leather boots made Skye a perfect match for her mount.

Champ's shiny bridle with blue brow band set off a leather-cut saddle with a poncho roll highlighting his glistening sorrel coat. A lather of sweat added to Champ's sparkle as he tossed his head and snorted, showing off the shiny red ribbon attached to his cheek strap.

"Way to go, Skye!" Mr. Chambers applauded.

Mrs. Chambers patted Champ's neck. "In that tough class, second place is something to be proud of."

"Awesome," Sooze said, holding Pepsi's lead chain.

Morgan's freckles smiled underneath her tan Stetson, her folded arms resting across the horn of her saddle. "I told you the gate would be no big deal."

"Yeah, thanks, guys." Skye glanced at the packed grandstand and back. "The only problem we had was the water obstacle. Did you see Champs pause and then step to the side just a little? I think that cost us the blue ribbon."

"Nonetheless, you did a great job," Mr. Chambers said. "By this time—"

"Attention, ladies and gentlemen," the loudspeaker blared through air that hinted of hay and horse manure, "all contestants for the Beginner's Showmanship Class please line up at the east gate. Calling all contestants for the next event, the Beginner's Showmanship Class."

Skye glanced at the grandstand again, looking for Chad. When she didn't see him, she focused back on

Sooze whose pallid face portrayed a strange mixture of panic and brazen courage.

Sandwiched between the horse and the fence, Sooze fussed with Pepsi's halter and arranged the horse's banded mane one last time. Sooze's blue Stetson sat squarely on top of her wig. A black necktie, red plaid shirt, jeans with a silver belt buckle, and black cowboy boots had totally changed her looks. Somehow, Sooze's painfully thin frame looked stunning. Pepsi's blood-red coat shimmered, and her black tail had been groomed to silky perfection.

"How do you feel?" Skye asked Sooze.

"Like I'm gonna throw up." Sooze made a face. "Not from the chemo. From my stomach doin' back flips."

Mrs. C. walked to Pepsi and checked the halter buckle. "All I can say is thank the Lord your treatment was in the middle of last week. It gave your body time to recuperate. You do feel strong enough to do this, don't you?" Mrs. Chambers looked into Sooze's eyes.

"I'm goin' in there if I have to crawl," Sooze said nervously.

Morgan laughed, stroking Blaze on the neck. "Hey, maybe you can start a Beginner's Turtle Class!"

A preoccupied Sooze shifted her attention to the gate. "I think I oughta go. They're all lining up."

"Let's say a quick prayer," Mr. Chambers said when he finished checking the last of Pepsi's hooves.

While Mr. C. prayed, Skye watched Sooze with half-closed eyes. Her stare never wavered from the ring.

A little prayer would help you right about now! Skye thought.

"Amen," Mr. Chambers finished. He and his wife backed away from Pepsi. "Now take your time, Sooze, and listen carefully to the judge."

"Yeah," Skye injected, "this is no time to be doing your own thing. Be cool."

"I don't have enough energy to do my own thing, thank you," Sooze joked while leading the horse away. "Pepsi will do her own thing, and we'll be back with a blue ribbon. You'll see."

"Careful, and don't rush!" Mrs. Chambers called.

"And try to get in the center, right in front of the judge when you line up," Morgan yelled. "Let him get a real good look at one gorgeous hunk of horse flesh!"

Sooze led Pepsi toward the gate at the other end of the corral. The big, bold number "17" on Sooze's back distinguished her from the rest of the intermingling pack.

"Five—no—six others," Skye said, pointing. She tugged the reins and turned Champ toward the ring. "A piece of cake for Pepsi."

Mrs. Chambers leaned over the top rail of the fence. "It all depends on Sooze. Pepsi's got the confirmation to win this class hands down, but I'm not sure Sooze is thinking straight. Tom, did you get a good look at her eyes? She's been into her pain pills again. I should have locked them up. This morning I noticed they're disappearing faster than cotton candy," she said seriously.

"Yeah, I noticed, too," Mr. Chambers agreed as he squared his Stetson. "This is no time to be taking a trip *without* your horse. I think she's going to learn a good lesson—but it breaks my heart."

"Look at her butting into the center of the pack!" Morgan said. "I didn't mean for her to do it *that* way. I bet she never even said excuse me."

Skye sighed and shook her head in agreement as she studied the contestants leading their horses single file into the show ring.

Pintos, grays, blacks, and browns, one prettier than the next, filed in, accompanied by contestants in a rainbow of Western attire. But no horse showed off its muscular perfection better than Keystone Stables' blue ribbon mare. Unfortunately, Pepsi Delight appeared to be led by a kid who staggered into the ring like her boots were stuck in mud.

"Something tells me this is *not* gonna be fun to watch." Skye frowned deeply. Like a cork in water, she bobbed on Champ's back as he stomped a front leg to shoo a fly.

Intermingled with a barrage of whinnies and billows of dust, the seven entries paraded single file into the ring. They walked, jogged, backed their horses, and finally squared them up in the center of the corral. By this time, Sooze had lost the center position to others who cleverly maneuvered their horses in front of her as she struggled to circle the ring. Now she found herself next to last as the judge started his close inspection at the other end of the line. As she had been trained to do, Sooze tugged on Pepsi's lead chain, prompting the horse to stand at attention. But ignoring the next step in her training, Sooze failed to check Pepsi's four legs. The front two lined up perfectly. The back two legs stood in a half stretch, the left one far ahead of the right. The horse's stance and perfect confirmation were thrown completely off.

"Sooze, check her back legs!" Skye yelled.

"Don't bother," Mrs. Chambers said. "We're too far away. I don't think she'd listen if she were standing right by this post. Sooze is in her own little world."

"Maybe before the judge gets to that end, she'll wake up and check the legs," Mr. Chambers said hopefully.

Morgan's despair rivaled all the others in the tightly knit group. "She's gonna blow it!"

Slowly the judge worked his way down the line, checking each horse's shape, eyeing it from the front, back, and sides, checking its teeth. In front of Pepsi, he raised his clipboard and pen just as Sooze yanked the lead chain. The sudden jerk sent Pepsi into a panic. She pranced in circles with Sooze frantically attempting to quiet her down. The judge stepped back in apparent frustration, and Skye could tell he was not at all amused.

"Uh, oh," Skye moaned. "Look at the judge's face."

Mr. Chambers raised his hat in frustration, scratched his head, and then squared his hat across his eyes. "Yep, she blew it all right. I know that judge, and he does not like to wait until you decide to square up your horse."

In minutes, the judge finished his tally. The loudspeaker announced the winners, the exit gate opened, and Sooze led Pepsi out and around the corral, returning to the Chambers empty-handed.

"That stupid judge!" Sooze yelled as she tied Pepsi to the fence. "He doesn't know good horseflesh when he sees it. He must be blind!"

Skye looked at Morgan and rolled her eyes. "Pepsi had every horse beaten without even blinking. *You* blew it— big time! You have to keep your horse still when the judge is standing right in front of you. Duh!"

"All right, you two," Mrs. Chambers interrupted. "It's over. No use crying over spilled milk. But, Sooze, we hope you have learned something important today. If you don't have your head screwed on right, even the simplest of tasks can defeat you. I think you know what I mean, don't you?"

"I didn't do nothing!" Sooze sassed. "It was all that stupid judge's fault!"

"Sooze, I think your day at the fair is over," Mrs. C. said sternly. "Tom and I are going to load the horses, and you'll be going home with me."

"Why?" Sooze questioned.

"You not only need to rest, but you need to get your head cleared," Mrs. Chambers added. "But the first thing you need is some food in your system."

"I'm not hungry!"

"Sooze," her foster mother said more emphatically, "you need something in your stomach. Now, while Tom and I load the horses, I'd like you to go get something to eat. We'll give you a half hour. Then come back here, and you'll ride home with me."

Skye dismounted her horse and handed the reins to Mr. Chambers. "Thanks, Dad," she said. "I could use a burger or something. Whatdaya say, Morgan?"

"Yeah, I could use something to eat too," Morgan glanced at the grandstand, "but I'm planning to meet some of the kids from church. They were sittin' on the top row a while ago. They must be on their way over here now."

Mr. Chambers retrieved Morgan's wheelchair from the truck and set it on a dirt-packed walkway that led from the show ring to the rest of the fairgrounds. Morgan handed Blaze's reins to Mrs. Chambers while Mr. Chambers loosened Morgan's legs from the Velcro safety strips on her saddle, gently slid her off into his arms, and placed her onto her Jazzy.

"Thanks," Morgan said, glancing at Skye and Sooze. "Hey, you two, come with me. Skye and I don't have to be back in a half hour, do we, Mrs. C.?"

"No, you have the rest of the afternoon," Mrs. Chambers said as she tied Blaze to the back of their hauling trailer. "Sooze is the only one who needs to go home."

"That's *so* not fair." Sooze whined.

"Duh. Life's not fair!" Skye said sarcastically. Then she added casually, "Hey, Morgan, is Chad here?"

"He was supposed to be, but I haven't seen him yet," Morgan replied and smiled, "so come with me, and maybe he'll join us along the way."

Sooze crowded herself next to Skye. "No, we'll do our own thing. Thank you."

An artificial smile masked Skye's regret at not getting to see Chad. "Sooze and I can grab something to eat, and then we'll meet you back here."

"Sounds good. Then we can do the fair thing with all the kids later, okay? Hey, here they come now." Morgan pointed across the field.

Sooze folded her arms angrily. "This stinks! You guys always get to have all the fun!"

Mrs. Chambers walked from the back of the trailer like she was stomping ants. "Sooze, it's time you learned that there are consequences for unwise decisions and actions. That's the way it's going to be," she said emphatically.

"Come on," Skye said to Sooze, tugging her arm, "you only have a half hour. Don't waste it arguing."

Mr. Chambers pulled a wallet from his back pocket. "Do you girls have enough money?"

"I do," Morgan answered. She moved ahead slowly. "Where else can I spend that megabucks allowance you give me?"

"I've got money," said Sooze.

"Me too," Skye answered. "So I guess we're outta here."

Morgan stopped in front of Skye, her troubled eyes reaching beyond her smiling face. "Skye," she pleaded, "don't you think you should go with *us?*"

Chapter Ten

"Well—" Skye hesitated. *I would like to see Chad,* she thought.

"Morgan, we don't need bodyguards," Sooze huffed. "Right, Skye?"

"Skye—" Mrs. Chambers' voice oozed with caution.

Mr. Chambers glanced back as he led Blaze to the trailer. "Remember, girls, you're on the honor system. We'll trust you as long as you don't give us any reason not to. And Sooze, you're already up to your neck in quicksand."

Morgan looked down the walkway. "Here come the guys now."

Sooze grabbed Skye's arm, abruptly pulling her away. "Come on. Let's go!"

"Later." Skye said to Morgan. *But I'd rather be going with you,* she thought. She glanced back at the three approaching friends. Each yelled hi and waved.

"Come on!" Sooze tugged Skye's sleeve harder. "We're history."

"All right! All right!" Skye yanked free. "Give me a break. I'm coming. See you later," she yelled warmly to the group.

The two girls soon blended into the bustling fairgrounds crowd, losing themselves among the buildings packed with antiques, arts and crafts, and farm gear. In the livestock section, pens and open barns overflowed with the commotion of prize calves, sheep, and pigs. Branching from the fair's core were narrow alleys blasting with music and hucksters begging passersby to, "Win a prize every time!"

Food stands, squeezed into every plot, satisfied the whims of an endless parade of empty stomachs. Sour barn smells faded into those of barbecued chicken, pizza, and funnel cakes. Skye's mouth watered as she peered down every lane for a stand that sold burgers and fries.

"Over there!" Skye zeroed in on the Bill's Buffalo Burgers stand. "I love those, and they have great curly fries!"

"I've got better things to do than eat," Sooze said, her dog-tired words sliding out from under her blue hat. "I've got a surprise for you."

"If it takes longer than twenty minutes, I'm not into it. Don't be any dumber than you've already been today. I'm gettin' a bison burger. What do you want?"

"Hey, I said I'm not hungry, and I mean it. Get what you want. Then we'll head over to the midway."

"Why? What's over there?" Skye asked as they walked toward the stand.

"Just wait and see." A silly smile flashed across Sooze's face.

"Don't tell me you wanna get on some rides! You already get sick to your stomach from the chemo. Besides, we don't have enough time."

"Just hurry up."

Skye ordered a burger, fries, and chocolate shake. While they headed for the midway, Sooze carried the box holding the fries and shake. Skye scarfed down her food and took long gulps from her thick creamy shake.

"This is too good." Her milky mustache confirmed her pleasure. "Want some?"

"Nope," Sooze said, balancing the cardboard tray while they weaved past a string of sideshows toward the Ferris wheel.

"Not that thing!" Skye griped through the last mouthful of food. She tossed the garbage in a trashcan, and then her eyes followed rotating buckets on the humongous light-flickering wheel. "I can't believe you want—" Skye glanced at her watch. "Sooze, we only have ten minutes to get back! I don't even have time to see the motorbikes!"

"Just cool it!" Sooze demanded. She took the lead on a walkway behind the wheel. "Come on down here behind the restrooms."

"What are you doing!"

"I see them. They're here!"

"Who?"

"Come on. You'll see."

Skye trailed after Sooze who puffed her way past the cinder-block bathroom building to a cluster of shady maples.

"Sooze!" *I am* so *gettin' bad vibes*, Skye thought. Her panic had nothing to do with the time.

"Hey, Sooze! Skye!" a voice bubbled from the shade of the trees. "Look at you two. Ride 'em cowboy! Where'd you get those rags?"

"Kenny, my man!" Sooze yelled, forcing her tired body toward the voice.

Skye squinted from the shade of her hat. She strained to focus on a couple of teenagers, one she didn't know. Beside the stranger stood a lanky boy who wore a green baseball cap flipped backward, a black T-shirt, and baggy jeans.

My old pill pal, Kenny Hartzell! Skye remembered him all too well. *What's he doin' here? He's supposed to be in lockup until November!*

As Sooze approached Kenny, his tattooed arms stretched to greet her with a high-five. Skye stepped forward and offered her own palms reluctantly.

"Hey, big man, what's happenin'?" Sooze asked.

"This is awesome seeing you guys again," Kenny said.

"You better believe it," Sooze said, her thumbs already up. She looked behind her as if she were hiding something.

Skye squared her hat smartly over her eyebrows and stared at Kenny. "How did you get out of Chesterfield? Weren't you supposed to be there for eighteen months?"

"Hey, I know how to buck the system." Kenny pointed to himself with his thumb. "I walked the line, and they let me out early. Simple as pie." His braces displayed a deceptive smile, and then he looked to the girl standing to his left.

"This is Tanya Bell," Kenny said. "She's from Philly."

Skye studied the girl who stood half a head taller than Kenny. Her smooth African-American face boasted two rows of perfect teeth and dimples that exploded when she smiled. An expensive looking red-and-white tank top and jean shorts hugged her shapely body, and her gazelle legs stood posed in high-heeled sandals. She easily could have passed for a model. She cradled an orange and white teddy bear at least half her size in one arm.

"Hey, what's up?" Sooze said to the girl.

"Tanya? Cool," Skye said. "What brings you to Snyder County? I mean, this is horse country—a long way from the big city. The closest we get to excitement is watching the sun go down."

"This is my sixth summer at the fair," Tanya said. "When I was younger, I visited some cousins who lived near here. I don't know," she said resting her free hand on her hip, "I just like it here. Things slow down just enough to let me think. I met Kenny last summer, and we've been friends ever since."

"Yeah," Kenny added, "real good friends. She stays with some people that live live a few doors down from us. Ain't that right?"

"Yeah," Tanya's dimples smiled.

91

"Awesome," Sooze said.

"Yeah," Skye said, looking at her watch. "Sooze, we've gotta go *now*."

"What's up?" Kenny asked. "Hey, that's right! You two are foster kids now! And you're hangin' out at the same pad. Does 'mommy' want you home?" he teased.

"You guys aren't serious," Tanya laughed. "You actually have rules that you have to follow?"

"Most of them aren't that bad," Skye said.

Sooze interrupted, "Kenny, did you know I have a brain tumor?"

"You're jerking my chain. For real?" he answered. He reached in his pocket to pull out a cigarette and lighter. He stuck the cigarette in his mouth and lit it. He held the pack out to Tanya, and she took one, holding it out for Kenny to light. Tanya took a long drag and directed a showy billow of smoke above her head.

"Yeah, I've had chemo and everything," Sooze started to explain. "This is a wig I'm—"

"Do you two wanna smoke?" Kenny interrupted.

"Sure," Sooze said. "I'm dyin' for one. It's been *forever*."

"Skye?" he asked.

"Ah—" Skye folded her arms.

Sooze rammed Skye with her elbow. "What's the matter with you? Our prison wardens ain't nowhere around. Go on. Relax and enjoy yourself."

"Nah," Skye said. "I don't even miss it."

"But I bet you really miss this kind of smoke." Kenny's eyebrows danced. "Ain't it about time you had a little fun?"

"Maybe you farmers don't know how to have a good time!" Tanya laughed.

"Come on," Sooze said sharply to Skye. "Just like old times."

Kenny stepped backward, pulling out a bulging, gray backpack from behind a large tree. "I got somethin' we can all enjoy in this heat." He opened the flap, pulled out a can of beer, and handed it to Tanya.

"Sooze," he said, pulling out another and tossing it to her.

She popped the seal and took a long guzzle of the foaming liquid.

"Skye," he said, flipping another can into her unsuspecting arms.

Skye juggled it, barely saving it from landing on the ground.

"Bottoms up, tough girl!" Tanya taunted. She popped open her tab and took a long drink.

Skye reluctantly popped the tab and took a mouthful. As soon as Skye swallowed, her whole body cringed with a feeling she couldn't explain. She had tasted alcohol dozens of times, but this was different. Her mind taunted her in a wave of strange, new guilt.

"After you accept Christ, God is with you all the time," Dad Chambers had said in devotions a few weeks ago. "He is there to help you make the right choices. When you sin, you grieve the Lord, and you'll feel terrible."

Skye's stomach recoiled as if she had been kicked by a horse, and she stiffened in shame. A Bible verse from

Pastor Newman's last sermon swept through her mind, haunting her with a new realization: *Therefore, if anyone is in Christ, he is a new creation; the old has gone, the new has come!*

She was no longer the same person she had been before becoming a Christian. A wave of nausea swept over her, and her eyes searched desperately for a garbage can to throw away the beer.

This is so *not fun,* Skye thought, her stomach churning.

"Hey, you guys—"

"Skye Nicholson!"

Like a carefully aimed bullet, the voice shot through the air, down the walkway, and hit Skye right in the middle of her unsuspecting back. Suddenly, she felt sick for two reasons. It was a familiar voice. A very familiar voice.

Chapter Eleven

Sooze wasn't the only one to be grounded. Back home, Mrs. Chambers' blue eyes flashed at the emergency family conference.

"It's very interesting what the Lord allowed me to see," Mrs. C. said. "I walked out of the administration office after finishing some horse business and—bam! There you two were under the trees. I certainly wasn't spying on you. I just happened to be at the right place at the right time."

Skye thought she'd die from not seeing Champ for two weeks. Worse than that, she had other feelings to deal with. She felt dirty inside; she had disappointed God. For days, she moped around the house while Sooze made light of their predicament and schemed her next move. Not until Skye, in the privacy of her bedroom, asked God to forgive her did she even come close to feeling right again. This being-a-Christian thing was serious business, and she had found out the hard way.

September came and with it Skye's freedom and the excitement of a new year at Madison Middle School. She also found herself more excited about spiritual things, soaking up Pastor Newman's sermons and Mr. Chambers' devotions. She read her own Bible and prayed every morning before facing the day and had a new determination to live for the Lord. She was also growing in her confidence that any challenge could be faced because she and God were going to school arm in arm.

Skye saw Sooze very little during the day, not only because they shared no classes together, but also because Skye had new interests. The old temptations were still there, but now she was making new friends, especially those in the youth group, and she had even decided to join a few clubs. At home, Skye did spend time with Sooze, mostly to help her with her homework and to support her through her declining health and medical treatments.

October in Pennsylvania brought crystal blue skies and rolling hills blanketed with palettes of brilliant colors. With the fall youth retreat only a day away, Skye and Sooze rode their horses to Piney Hollow after school to help Mr. Chambers clean up. He was busy cutting the weeds around the campsite when Skye and Sooze rode up to join him.

"Hi, girls," Mr. Chambers acknowledged, turning off the mower and wiping his forehead. "What a beautiful day to work outside. This nice breeze is just right to cool off a hot cowboy. Thanks for volunteering to help me get this place in shape."

"Did we have a choice?" Skye giggled. She patted Champ and feasted her eyes on the blazing fall colors. "Just kidding."

"I'm too tired," Sooze said.

"And I don't think she *is* kidding," Skye added.

Mr. Chambers bent down and checked the gas level of the lawn mower. "Sooze, we know you have very little energy because of your treatments. I don't expect you to do much here. Just hand Skye the things she needs while she scrubs out the chuck wagon. You can give her moral support. Tie your mounts in the shade over there. We have a lot of work to do."

The girls maneuvered their horses to a hitching post under large scrub pine branches.

"Man, I hate to clean," Skye said to Sooze, "but this kind of cleaning isn't bad, out in the open and around the horses. Why don't you just sit and watch and keep me company. I can tell you're feelin' pretty bad."

Skye dismounted and tied Champ to the railing. Leaning against the post, she yanked the strap open on her hard hat and slipped it off. Her hair blew freely in the breeze.

Sooze slipped the hard hat off her bald head and put on a red baseball cap that she had pulled from a saddlebag. Her body looked like the twin of the Pillsbury Doughboy, bloated from the steroids they had been giving her to build up her strength. She moved like she had cement in her boots, and even the simple task of securing Pepsi's reins was a struggle.

"I only threw up once this morning," she said in a heavy breath. "It's been almost a week since my last chemo."

Skye balanced her hat on the saddle's horn and tied her hair into a ponytail with a rubber band. "You sure don't look like *you* all puffed up like a balloon. But I guess the steroids do help give you a little energy, don't they?"

"Yeah, about two ounces worth—one for each little finger," Sooze tried to joke.

"Well, I guess even that little bit helps."

Skye walked to the truck bed, where she filled two buckets with hot water from a large container. She poured Lysol into one bucket and grabbed a fistful of rags and shoved them into her jean pockets. Sooze had followed her over to the truck, but one look into her foster sister's eyes gave Skye a start. Sooze looked so tired.

"Here, you carry these and the broom." Skye yanked the rags from her pocket, handed them to Sooze, and picked up both buckets of water. "Victory over spiders!" she declared as she turned toward the chuck wagon.

While Mr. Chambers groomed the campsite, Skye swept out the wagon and scrubbed its insides. Sooze rested on a crate outside, handing Skye anything she needed. After retrieving fresh water and a batch of clean cloths, the girls sat inside the covered wagon. Sooze handed Skye cooking utensils and plastic containers one at a time while Skye scrubbed them clean. The late afternoon sun filtering through the tarp warmed the wagon, giving it a pale yellow tint. Whisks of crisp autumn air brought welcome relief from the strong smell of Lysol.

Sooze smiled impishly, thinking ahead to her next words. "This place is so awesome. Speaking of awesome," she slipped in casually, "I'm meeting Jason Stine third period tomorrow. He has some stuff for me."

"Jason Stine?" Skye's face clouded in disgust. "I was sure you'd put that behind you."

Sooze handed Skye a large metal ladle. "Well, our good buddy Kenny got himself busted again. This time when they locked him up in Chesterfield, they probably threw away the key. I needed a new contact, so Jason was more than willing. Do you wanna meet me fifth period in the gym bathroom? I can give you some stuff."

"Of course not," Skye said as she scrubbed the spoon in one bucket and then rinsed it in the second. She pulled it out and jabbed it in Sooze's direction with a very determined look. "I don't get why you're so set on making things worse for yourself."

Sooze grabbed the spoon and smothered it with a soggy towel. "What's it gonna do, kill me? I figure the tumor's going to do that first. So what if I use a little something to get me through this?"

"You have plenty to help you get through this, Sooze," Skye responded. "You have me, Morgan, the Chambers,

Pepsi, and God—if you would just give him a chance to show you that he can help."

"Skye, you're *so* different since you've been living here. I don't even know you anymore. They've really gotten to you, haven't they?"

"I told you before, Sooze, nobody *got* to me." Skye grabbed a bunch of utensils, plopped them in the soapy bucket, and started washing. "I've just learned so much about myself and God—and well—I needed him on my side. When I accepted Christ after our accident—we could have been killed, you know—it just changed the way I look at things. I don't need *stuff* to make me feel good anymore. God is always there when I need him. He's the best friend I've ever had."

One at a time, Skye handed over the utensils. Sooze dried and placed them on the counter behind her.

"You know we've been learning about drinking and drugs in youth group. Remember what Pastor Newman said? That stuff can really mess up your body."

"Nah, I don't remember nothin' from youth group, I'm usually in La-La Land. That church stuff isn't for me."

Skye whacked the bucket with a metal spoon in frustration. She wondered if she would ever be able to get through to her friend.

"Skye—" Sooze started to say.

Skye busied herself scrubbing an old tin coffee pot. "What?"

There was a long silence, which forced Skye to look up. Out from the shadow of the ball cap, steady streams of tears covered Sooze's face and dropped freely onto her sweatshirt.

"What's wrong?" Skye slowly pulled the pot from the rinse bucket and wrapped it in a cloth.

"Do you ever think about dying?" Sooze cried.

"Sure. Sometimes. Doesn't everyone?"

"No, I mean really dying—like now." Sooze dried her eyes with the already drenched towel. "The doctors keep telling me that I'm okay, but I've got a bad feeling about this. I don't think I'm gonna make it, and I don't know what's out there."

For once, Skye was speechless.

"I feel so alone," Sooze added.

"You have your mom . . . and all of us!" Skye spoke with more hope than she was feeling.

"How many times has *Mom* come to see me since I've been here?" Sooze's voice rose in anger. "In fact, how many times has she even called?"

Skye glanced upward, knowing the answer.

"That's right," Sooze said. "Zero! Nada! Zilch! She doesn't care. She never did."

"But you have us," Skye said. "And Pastor Newman and the people at church care. Everyone is praying for you."

"That doesn't help much when I'm lying in bed at night thinking about—Do you really think there's a heaven?"

"Yes," Skye said strongly. "The Bible says there is."

"Then you don't just die like a dog," Sooze sniffled. "I mean, you go somewhere, don't you?"

"Yes. Everyone who accepts Christ goes to be with him. It couldn't be much simpler. And it's wonderful there. No more crying. No more pain. Sooze, why don't you give your heart to God? Then you wouldn't have to worry about dying because you'd know you'd go to heaven."

"I've never thought much about it," Sooze said softly. "You heard my mom when we went to see her. She has no time for God. She always said we could make it on our own. I don't think she even believes he exists. I think part of her problem is that we know some people who say they're religious and all, but they have this long list of rules they try not to break. They live like they're in prison all the time."

"I'll tell you one thing, Sooze. I never thought about him much either before I came here. All I thought about was livin' it up, but I was so messed up from all the rotten things I had done. The truth is that I was having a lousy time instead of a good time. This God stuff all makes perfect sense to me now. I know that when I die, I'll go to be with Jesus. That is so cool. Why don't you give him a chance?"

"I'll think about it," Sooze said quietly.

"Hey, girls," Mr. Chambers said, popping his head into the back of the wagon. He glanced at his watch and then took in what the two girls had accomplished. "Wow! It looks and smells great in here. We've finally got a decent campsite. Why, I think I could eat off this floor. Great job, ladies! Let's pack up and head back for supper!"

Chapter Twelve

"Beth, over here!" Skye said as she stood near one corner of the barn loft.

Around Skye, the youth group girls chattered like birds, claiming their cherished spots to spend the night. The bed of hay quickly vanished under a sea of sleeping bags, backpacks, and boom boxes. The air pulsated with jokes, the latest school news, and the excitement of roughing it at Keystone Stables.

"Girls!" Mr. Chambers called from the bottom of the stairs. "Hay Wagon Number One leaving the station in five minutes."

"Hey, Melissa!" Skye yelled at a tall blond, tiptoeing across the sleeping bags toward the steps. "Come here."

"What's up?" Melissa walked over to Skye who met her halfway.

"Is Chad here? I didn't see him get off the bus."

"Yeah, he's here. He was in the back, protecting his guitar from the wild beasts." Melissa flashed her pretty smile and studied Skye from head to toe. "Although—the way you look, he'll have a hard time keeping his eyes on his guitar. Your dark hair looks terrific with that red sweatshirt. And where'd you get those hikers?"

"At the mall." Skye ran her fingers through her silky hair, letting it fall casually onto her shoulders. "It's too cool that Madison's colors are red and gray. I always thought I looked okay in red."

"Okay is not the word," Melissa said. "More like awesome! Chad will be totally impressed."

The girls giggled their way into the flow of those who were already starting down the stairs. At the bottom, they joined one of the chaperones, Mr. Salem, and the boys who were meandering to each stall, looking at the horses, reaching cautiously to pet their noses. Skye made a beeline toward Champ, bubbling about how great a horse he was.

"Okay, kids!" Mr. Chambers shouted from the open doorway. "Wagon departing!"

Like thirsty cows running to a watering hole, the kids charged toward the door. Mr. Chambers barely managed to get out of the way before they rushed through the opening and jumped onto an open wagon fluffed with a soft bed of hay. Against the back railings, Morgan and Sooze already sat like two hens on a nest of eggs. The last ones to board were the chaperone and Skye, who found herself sitting near Chad. As usual when he was around, her face turned red hot.

Chad's brown eyes sparkled. "Hey, Skye!" he said.

"Hey," she said back. "Where's your guitar?"

"On the driver's seat with Mr. Chambers," he answered. His chipmunk smile and curly blond eyelashes seemed to light up the wagon. "I didn't want it smashed in the hay fight that I predict will happen with this bunch. So, how's it goin'?"

"Good. It's goin' good," she answered.

For the next hour, the wagon drawn by two work-horses from a neighboring farm meandered on dirt roads around and through the Keystone Stables property. On the hill behind the barn, the passengers enjoyed the beauty of autumn in Shade Valley that stretched for miles around them. The wagon passed the picnic grove, the pond, and crept through the red and orange canopy toward Piney Hollow.

Bouncing with every rut and bump in the road, the group laughed, sang choruses, shared stories from school, and talked about football and soccer. Despite the excitement of it all, Skye found herself preoccupied with thoughts of Chad as she stared awkwardly at her boots, not knowing what to say to him.

Deep in thought, Skye hardly noticed the hay fight that had erupted until a wad of it hit her right in the face. She gasped and sputtered like a motorbike out of gas, spitting out hay dust. Then all in one motion she scooped up a handful of hay and pitched it toward the first target in her line of fire—Chad. Her reward was a handful of itchy hay dust down her sweaty back.

The wagon bounced along the trail with squeals of laughter and a dustbowl of flying hay. When it rounded the corner through the woods and pulled into Piney Hollow, Mrs. Chambers and Mrs. Salem were placing heaps of food on a large table in front of the chuck wagon. With the smell of hot dogs, baked potatoes, and roasted corn in the crisp fall air, the hay fight ended as fast as it had started.

The kids jumped off the wagon, dusted each other off, and gathered in a circle as Mr. Salem led them in prayer. Shoving each other in line, they filled their plates with the best that Piney Hollow's chuck wagon could offer and sat on sawed-off stumps around the campfire.

Skye, Robin, Sooze, and Morgan sat in a cluster eyeing Chad and Bobby, who were engaged in a corn-eating contest. By the time supper came to a side-splitting end, Pastor Newman pulled up in an RV. After a quick cup of coffee, he presented a short challenge to the group at the chapel. A question-and-answer period about the book of Jonah followed. Then the group was dismissed for some time to socialize.

Chad and Skye made their way back to the campfire. Chad poked at a cluster of coals in the fading flames.

"Pastor Newman sure knows his stuff. I always wondered why Jonah was so mad at God for sending him to Nineveh," he said. "I guess those Ninevites weren't exactly your friendly next-door neighbors. They would've chopped your head off pretty quick."

Skye grabbed a hotdog stick and stuck a marshmallow on the end. "Yeah, it does make more sense now. I always thought that story was a fairy tale. But a big fish really *did* swallow Jonah. Can you imagine being in a fish's stomach? Phew!"

They were both laughing when Sooze approached and sat down next to Skye.

"Hi, Sooze," Skye said with more enthusiasm than she actually felt. *This is* so *not the time to be crashing the party, Sooze!* she thought ungratefully.

Chad looked over past Skye. "Hey, Sooze, how you doin'?"

"So-so," Sooze forced out.

Skye smiled weakly.

Sooze smiled back. "Skye, I need to talk to you."

Skye ignored her and turned to Chad. "Bobby told me you just got hired at Jacob's Hardware Store."

Chad smiled. "Yeah, I'm saving for a car."

"Skye," Sooze said softly.

Skye turned toward Sooze and gave her a can-this-possibly-wait look. "What!"

"I *really* need to talk to you—now."

Without wanting to, Skye noticed Sooze's posture—slumped over, the brim of her Stetson pulled down, tears dropping on her shirt.

"Chad, I'm sorry." Skye was already turning toward Sooze.

"No problem," Chad threw his stick in the fire and stood. "I'll go see what the guys are doing."

"Okay, everybody!" Mr. Chambers announced right behind Skye. "Time for the scavenger hunt! Meet me over by the hitching post under the pines!"

"Scavenger hunt?" Chad responded. "It's almost dark!"

Mr. Chambers' mustache twitched playfully. "I know, my good man. That's what makes it so much fun. Trying to find an acorn with the sun sinking fast in the west is very tricky. But, at least the bears usually don't come out until after dark."

"Bears?" Chad's smile melted into mock fear.

"Ah, he's just kidding," someone called out. But the tone didn't sound reassuring.

"I sure hope so!" Chad's glance swept the scene. "Whatever, I'm ready. Let's go—and in the opposite direction of the bears!"

"Are you two coming?" Mr. Chambers asked.

"In a sec," Skye said. "We have to do something first."

"Fine," Mr. Chambers said with an understanding smile. He joined Chad and walked to where the others were gathering.

Skye knelt beside Sooze. "What is it?" Skye whispered.

"I need ta talk to you," Sooze's voice quivered. "Alone."

"How about over there," Skye pointed toward the chapel. "There's nobody around."

The girls walked to the bench in front of the cross. Sooze sat in obvious pain, gasping for breath. Then she started to weep out loud.

Skye sat down next to Sooze and slipped an arm around her. "Did somebody say somethin'?"

"It's nothin' like that," Sooze said, wiping her nose on her sleeve. She glanced toward the cross. "All that stuff about God you've told me since I moved in here—it finally sank in tonight when I listened to Pastor Newman. I mean it really sank in. I wanna invite Jesus Christ into my life, and I'm not just sayin' that 'cause I'm scared. I see now that I've been fighting against myself."

"Sooze, God loves kids like us. That's what's so neat about him. Jesus died so we could be at peace here on Earth and live with him forever someday in heaven."

Sooze studied the cross. "Well, what do I have to do? I've never belonged to a church. Do I have to join? I've never even prayed. How do I pray?"

"Just do what I did. It's not that hard, Sooze. Ask God right now to forgive you and wash away your sins. Jesus already took your punishment, so there's nothing for you to do but thank him for it and accept it. Just talk to him honestly. That's all he wants."

Unaware of the yells and laughter from the woods, the two friends talked and prayed. A sliver of pink from the setting sun found its way through the trees, illuminating the cross as the two bowed their heads. For the first time in her life, Sooze prayed out loud. Opening her heart wide before God, she asked him to forgive her and to come into her life.

"Amen." Sooze said with a relieved tone in her voice.

"Sooze," Skye said, looking into her friend's eyes, "God just made you brand new on the inside. You'll never be the same again. You'll see."

The friends threw their arms around each other and cried tears of joy.

Chapter Thirteen

e're going to a football game," Mrs. Chambers shouted above the noise and laughter of the TV in the Bodmer living room. "Sooze asked if we could stop by for a few minutes to see you."

Skye and Sooze plopped down on the floor and gave Mrs. Chambers the green chair. With November's chill and the threat of snow, all three were bundled up in heavy coats, on their way to Madison's last game.

Mrs. Bodmer had already nestled into her favorite spot on the sofa hours earlier. Her frizzy hair was now red. Purple fingernails fondled a cigarette that found its way to her lips every few seconds. The room looked even more crowded than before.

Sooze's mother lifted the remote control from her belly and forced herself to click the TV off. "I was wonderin' what brought you this way. I hope this ain't nothin' more than a social call." Her stare jumped to Sooze. "And ain't you a pretty sight. Whatcha been eatin' to get

111

so big so fast? You'll soon be as big as me, and that's sayin' something!"

"It's not from food, Mom," Sooze said. "It's from my meds."

"What meds?" she asked flippantly.

"Steroids," Skye said. "They help her fight the pain from the tumor."

Mrs. Chambers shifted her weight. "Sooze's medicines do strange things to her body, Mrs. Bodmer. But we didn't come to talk about that. Sooze wants to tell you something."

"What trouble are you in now?" Mrs. Bodmer snarled.

"I'm not in any trouble at all," Sooze replied calmly.

"This time Sooze has *good* news to tell you, if you can believe it!" Skye could not keep the delight from her voice.

Mrs. Chambers added, "She's been making some very good choices in her life lately, and I think she should tell you about them herself. Go on, Sooze."

Mrs. Bodmer took a drag on her cigarette, blew the smoke up over her head, and crossed her arms. "Well, what is it?" She stared glumly at her daughter.

Sooze leaned forward slowly and rested her elbows on her knees. "I've been learning all kinds of stuff at the Chambers' house, Mom, to help me get my head together. They've been telling me about God, and a few weeks ago, I asked Jesus Christ to come into my life."

"And what in corn's sake does that mean?" Mrs. Bodmer barked, running her free hand through her frizz.

"Don't tell me you got religion now! That's all I need to hear!"

"It's not religion, Mrs. Bodmer," Mrs. Chambers said. "It's a personal relationship with God—the creator of the universe. When someone accepts what Christ did for us on the cross as Sooze did, God makes that person new, inside and out. Sooze is a different person now."

"Yeah," Skye added. "I accepted Christ too, and I've only been in trouble once since then. God gives—"

"Hey!" Mrs. Bodmer snapped. "I told you the last time that I didn't wanna hear any of this God junk. My kid still got that tumor in her head? Huh? Look how much good God's doin' her! Now if that's all you came to talk about, there's the door!"

"But, Mom," Sooze pleaded, "you don't understand. This is different. If you'd just listen."

"That's it! No more. You got no business comin' into *my* house and crammin' this religion stuff down my throat." Mrs. Bodmer blew a short blast of smoke out her nose and scowled at Sooze. "And I'm surprised at you for fallin' for this baloney, Susan. What's the matter with you?"

"Mom," Sooze's voice cracked, "God is real—and—he loves you!"

"Easy, Sooze," Mrs. Chambers warned.

"Yeah, and pigs can fly!" Mrs. Bodmer's face turned beat red. "If that's all you came to tell me, I ain't inter-ested. Let me repeat it, so it's nice and clear. I ain't interested! Period!"

"I'm sorry to hear that." Mrs. Chambers stood and zipped her coat. "All right, girls, I think it's time to go. But, Mrs. Bodmer, would you consider doing one thing for Sooze?"

"What?" Mrs. Bodmer said gruffly.

"Thanksgiving is in a few weeks. Would you come to our place for dinner? We'll have turkey and all the trimmings. If you like football, Tom will have games on all afternoon."

"Yeah," Skye agreed. "We'd love to have you. Wouldn't we, Sooze?"

"Please, Mom. I could show you my bedroom and the barn and the horse I ride."

"We'll even come and pick you up," Mrs. Chambers added.

"I'm busy!" Mrs. Bodmer fired back.

"We were never busy before on Thanksgiving," Sooze said. "We always ate frozen dinners and watched TV. What's different this year?"

"I told you I'm busy. Thanks, but no thanks," Mrs. Bodmer clicked on the TV.

"Then how about Christmas?" Mrs. C. said loudly.

"I'm busy!" Mrs. Bodmer said even louder without thinking twice. "I'm just busy!"

Skye and Sooze followed Mrs. Chambers into the back of the Booster Club stand at the football stadium. Wrapped in a red apron, Mr. Chambers stood at the stoves and labored over French fries bubbling in troughs of hot grease. Morgan sat in a corner peeling potatoes. Two adults at the front counter were selling fries like they were made of gold.

"Hey, it's about time you got here to help." Mr. Chambers smiled when he saw his wife. "I'm just about fried out. I'd give a month's salary for a hot dog right about now."

"You poor man," his wife kidded. "How you suffer for such a just cause as new band uniforms. Give me your apron, and you can go round up a hot dog. How about making that two!"

"Make it three!" Morgan laughed.

Mr. Chambers took off his apron and handed it to his wife before turning toward Sooze and Skye. "Girls, do you want a hot dog, too? I might as well make it a half dozen."

The girls traded mischievous glances. "Nah," Skye said. "We're wondering if we could go get somethin' to eat on our own. We'd like to hike around the field for a while. Maybe we'll see some kids from Youth for Truth. That's really what football games are for. Right?"

Mr. and Mrs. Chambers laughed, and Mr. C. walked toward the door.

"Well, in my day," he said, "let's see, that was about a hundred years ago, we went to football games to watch the players make fools of themselves chasing that pigskin all around the field. I guess times have changed, haven't they, dear?"

Mrs. Chambers took her coat off, slipped the apron over her head, and tied it behind her back. She smiled affectionately at her husband. "You just don't know us girls, Tom. We go to games for things other than sitting and watching what happens to some dumb football on a field. Right, girls?"

"Right!" Skye answered.

"Right!" Sooze agreed.

Morgan pointed at the stove. "I'd rather peel potatoes next to these warm fryers any day than go out there and turn into an ice cube. Sitting in those cold bleachers just doesn't appeal to a lightweight like me. Don't forget my hot dog, Mr. C.—and that's with everything."

Tom Chambers grabbed his coat off a hook on the wall. "Three hot dogs with the works, coming right up!"

Skye gave Sooze a sheepish grin. "We'll just walk around and see if anybody from youth group is here."

"Oh, they're here," Morgan said. "They were hangin' around just a few minutes ago. All except Chad. He's working tonight."

Too bad, Skye thought, but she hid her disappointment. "Well, we'll look for the other kids if Sooze feels all right," Skye said it as if she didn't have a clue who Chad was.

"Yeah, no problem as long as we turtle walk," Sooze said, embarrassment peeking through each word. "I know I can make it around the field at least once. We're outta here."

Mr. Chambers made a mad dash toward the hot dog stand, and the two girls headed off in the opposite direction. Skye took short steps to match Sooze's snail pace. They weaved around scrambling children and adults who carried cartons overflowing with food. After only half a lap, Sooze puffed like she had just run the last touchdown. They stopped near one of the goal posts "to watch the game," or so Skye said.

"Hey, Sooze! Can you believe it? Madison is winning, fourteen to zip! I thought they were supposed to lose tonight." A sharp gust of frigid air swept through the stadium, forcing Skye's hands into her jean pockets.

"Awesome!" Sooze said. "Robin told me in school today that it's been five years since we beat Lewisburg. If they pull this one off, it'll be party time."

Skye glanced at Sooze who was pulling her baseball cap down tighter over her wig and shoving her hands into her own deep pockets.

As if a gigantic snow bucket in the sky had overturned, large fluffy snowflakes began to tumble from the pitch-black sky. Dancing to Madison's band, they swirled and bounced in front of the brilliant lights, dropping a curtain of white that easily distracted Skye's attention from what was happening on the field.

"Hey, it's snowin'!" Skye could hardly contain her excitement.

"This is too awesome!" Sooze said, joy overshadowing her pain. "I love when it snows. Hey, ever go snowboarding?"

"No, but I've gone sledding a zillion times." In the same breath, Skye's next question cut to the heart of her deepest thoughts. "Sooze, ever think you could live with your mom again?"

"I don't know," Sooze's thoughts were far away. "I used to hate her, but I found out tonight that I don't anymore. I don't like her yet, but I don't hate her either. She needs God worse than I did."

A large roar echoed through the stadium, and the Madison Musketeer Band blasted their victory song.

"Hey, we just scored!" Skye said. The girls started walking again. "You gotta admit we were, like, total losers. But the Chambers never trashed us. Neither did God. I think we oughta be prayin' for your mom more than ever."

"I'm praying as hard as I can," Sooze added. Then suddenly pointing to the back of the bleachers, she yelled out, "There's Jason!"

"Sooze, you didn't tell me you wanted to meet *him* here!" Skye's disappointment went unnoticed. "Come on. Let's go find the other kids."

"One momento," Sooze said, forcing her body to move at a pace she had not been able to muster for some time.

"Unreal," Skye grumbled, trailing after Sooze who hurried into Jason's shadow.

Jason's bleached orange and green hair stuck out like it had frozen that way. Each ear had a lineup of three earrings. Despite the cold, his scrawny body was clad in

only a short-sleeved black T-shirt with a decal of a ram's head snorting fire and baggy cargo pants that smothered his feet and bunched on the ground.

"Sooze, babe. Good to see you. What can I get for you tonight?" Jason's smile flashed with eagerness as his hands slipped into his pockets. "I've got bags overflowing with any little thing your heart desires." He gave Skye the once over. "And you brought your friend along."

Skye grabbed Sooze's coat sleeve. "Sooze, let's go."

"Wait!" Sooze said sharply. "I've got somethin' I gotta do here."

"Sooze!" Skye said double sharply.

"I said wait a minute!"

"Yeah, what's the hurry, gorgeous?" Jason sneered. "We're just ready to start the party!"

"Not me! Not this time!" Skye said, turning. "I'll wait for you over there by the fence."

If the snow had been falling in buckets before, it was falling by the truckloads now. Skye had just barely turned toward the bleachers and now strained to see past the onslaught of flakes. "Sooze, don't do this!" Skye said, scarcely aware that she had just started a conversation with herself. "You'll be sorry."

By now the frigid air ran through Skye's veins like ice water. The snow quickly formed a thin blanket on the field, adding a chill that made Skye feel like she was standing on an iceberg. Skye wished she were home. She moved her feet and wiggled her toes, trying to get them warm.

"Come on, Sooze!" she grumbled. "I bet that dumb football would listen before you would."

The words flying between Jason and Sooze lasted longer than Skye thought *she* could. But, strangely, Skye noticed that no bags, large or small, passed between them. In fact, Sooze's hands never left her pockets. Finally, Sooze left Jason standing alone, scratching his head of frozen stiff hair.

"I told him to chill out," Sooze labored to say as she joined Skye. She let out a slight giggle. "Hey, get it? Snow, cold, *chill*? Anyway, I don't need that stuff anymore. Not since I've got God on my side."

Despite the cold, Skye managed a relieved smile. "I was afraid—"

"Yeah, I know," Sooze said. "C'mon, let's go find our *real* friends."

A thunderous cheer erupted from the Madison crowd, and the band played their victory march one more time. But Skye and Sooze had other things on their minds. They slowly walked away.

Chapter Fourteen

I never thought about buying gifts for anyone but me," Sooze forced her words out as she and Morgan maneuvered their wheelchairs through the crowded mall. For a month now, Sooze had begun to depend on her own Jazzy when she had to travel a considerable distance. "Christmas was always just an excuse for Mom to get plastered. The rest of the family never bothered with us much, so holidays were no big deal. Chuck and I usually just watched TV or ran around. I guess my running around days are over."

Skye followed closely, making sure that their three winter coats and the packages overhanging in the girls' baskets stayed put.

"Wait a sec, you two," Skye said, saving a bag from tumbling to the ground. "I need to fix some things back here. Pull over."

After Skye had rearranged the cargo, the wheelchairs resumed, crawling like a pair of gigantic snails, trying their best to avoid distracted shoppers. Skye trailed behind and tried to balance bags that still had a mind of their own.

"Your running around days might be over, but not your running *over* days," Skye said. "This place is packed. It's a miracle that you two haven't mowed down some poor shopper along the way."

"I have enough to worry about without being sued for reckless driving!" Sooze managed a giggle. "We just have to be extra careful, or some kid could lose his toes. Right, Morgan?"

"Right!" Morgan spun her chair around and took a long look at the line of stores on the other side of the mall. "I just love Christmas! What are you two buying Mr. and Mrs. C.? It's only a few weeks until the big day!"

Excitement over celebrating her first Christmas as a Christian had Skye practically jumping out of her skin, especially the part about buying gifts for people she loved.

"I've noticed Mom's Bible is pretty ragged," Skye said. "I think I'll get her a new one—I'm thinkin' something fancy with a burgundy leather cover."

"How about Mr. C.?" Morgan asked.

"Wait 'til you hear this! I saw the neatest little mustache grooming kit. It's perfect."

Sooze adjusted the baseball cap that covered her wig. "I was thinkin' about a sentimental gift for Mr. C. I thought maybe a new key chain with his initials, and a crazy visor for the new truck would be cool. Kind of a belated 'I'm really sorry for wrecking your truck' gift. What do ya think?"

Skye studied her friend's eyes that betrayed dog tiredness and persistent pain. "Sooze, you okay? We can go now if you're too tired."

"Not a chance," Sooze answered. "I've got to find a bright blue scarf for Mrs. C. to go with her western duds."

"Brilliant," Morgan said, brushing back her kinky red hair. "I've been saving for months for what I'd like to get them. Did you know their twentieth anniversary is next month? I saw the neatest wall clock with tiny running horses on it. They'll love it."

Skye thought of something special she had seen in a store the week before, and her heart played leap frog. *That's right!*

"Hey, now that we're talking horses, I know somethin' we could all get them, and it wouldn't cost us megabucks. Off to the toy store!"

Sooze scrunched her face like she was sucking lemons. "The toy store?"

Morgan laughed. "Okay, Skye, if you say so. But I'm guessin' you've lost your mind."

"Stay with me. You'll see!" Skye promised.

The girls giggled their way to the other end of the mall, excused themselves past other shoppers, and finally approached the window of the Just Kidding toy store.

"Feast your eyes on those!" Skye bubbled as they lined up in front of the store window.

Horse models of all shapes and sizes posed in prances or were rearing on their powerful hind legs. The horses stood around a red barn on a green grass-like carpet, and a small white fence encircled the entire display. Above the exquisite models hung a wooden plaque carved with the word "BREYER."

"Wow!" Morgan said as she stared at the display. "I've seen some of these horses before, but never in a spread like this!"

"This is awesome!" Sooze said.

"Check it out," Skye said, her voice rising to a higher pitch. "There's one in there for every horse at Keystone. Look—there in the back on the left. That one's just like Champ!"

Sooze pointed to another corner. "Hey, there's Blaze! Look, Morgan, its legs are black just like hers!"

Morgan leaned forward in her chair. "Yeah, I see it. Do you see Pepsi anywhere?"

"Yeah," Skye answered, "next to the black stallion. If I didn't know better, I would've thought they used Pepsi's picture to make that horse. It looks like her twin."

"This is too sweet," Sooze said. "Oh, I get it, Skye."

"Me too," Morgan added.

Skye's whole face sparkled with a smile. "It won't cost that much if we all pool our money. We could get both Mom and Dad a model of their horse. Over there in the right corner is Chief. Do you see him?"

"Yep," Sooze said.

"Unreal," Morgan said. "That model is even the same pinto colors as Chief. They'll love these! Let's do it."

Sooze backed away from the window and bowed her head. Her swollen fingers played with each other.

Skye followed Sooze's reaction. "What's the matter?"

"Do you feel sick?" Morgan added.

Sooze looked up and stared at the window. "Nah, nothin' like that. Since I'm not getting chemo, I'm not sick anymore. Just tired. I told you before I never bought a gift for anybody in my whole life. That includes my mother. Not for any reason. Not even her birthday. She collects things like this. You should see our one bedroom upstairs. She has ceramics and dolls and plastic animals sitting all over the place. I bet she'd like one of these. I could get her the one that looks like Pepsi."

"How could she *not* love it? That's a super idea," Skye said.

Morgan turned her chair toward the entrance. "C'mon," she said, with a smile as big as Skye's, "let's go spend some money!"

The busy weeks before Christmas brought the sights and smells that heralded the joy of the long-awaited holiday. Shade Valley now glistened with several inches of freshly fallen snow, adding to the season's delight. The spirit of giving to honor Christ's birth seemed to reach into even the darkest corners of every home, igniting them with lights of hope displayed in brilliant color. Yet, the beauty of the Christmas season somehow sent a more somber message to the family at Keystone Stables. Though prayers for Sooze had been going up constantly, it had become too clear that five months of treatments were not helping Sooze. She was gravely ill.

Shortly after the girls' shopping trip, Sooze's physical condition weakened so fast that she was no longer able to even sit up. Mr. and Mrs. Chambers had stationed a hospice bed for her in their living room where a fresh towering spruce tree twinkled in one corner. White lights around the bay window cast a soft glow in the room and on the snow-covered shrubs outside.

Skye and Morgan's spare moments always brought them to their friend whom they had grown to love. Every evening they ate their meals at her bedside, encouraging her, relating the news of the day, telling her silly jokes, reading to her from the Bible, and praying with her before she fell asleep. Sooze grew weaker and thinner. Much of the time, her meds kept her in a deep sleep. When she was awake, it took all her strength to manage a few words. But she could smile, and when she did, it illuminated her entire face.

It was Christmas Eve, and snowflakes fell like tiny cotton balls on an already sparkling winter wonderland. Skye and Mr. Chambers had finished their barn chores, and Mrs. Chambers and Morgan had just done the dishes when Pastor Newman stopped by.

The family gathered around Sooze's bed and sang Christmas carols. After Pastor Newman prayed and left, Skye and Morgan decided to wrap the last few gifts at the dining room table. Mr. and Mrs. Chambers reclaimed their chairs next to Sooze. A Christmas CD played softly in the background as the scent of cinnamon wafted through the air.

Skye wrapped gold ribbon around a shiny green package. Her head throbbed from endless crying, and her throat ached. *I know God does miracles. He healed Dad*, she told herself. *And he just has to do another miracle now.*

"Do you think God could heal her?" Skye asked Morgan. "I mean, she's been fighting so hard."

"I don't know what to say," Morgan replied as she taped a box shut. "Mrs. C. says that God's ways are not our ways."

"It doesn't even seem like Christmas, does it?" Skye felt her throat tighten again and her eyes tear up. "I mean, how can we be happy at a time like this?"

Morgan pushed the box she was wrapping to the center of the table. "I know. This is the worst thing I've ever gone through."

"I just don't get it." Skye looked up into Morgan's glistening eyes.

"Skye, can't you see that God sent Sooze here, so she would come to know him? She's going to a far better place than we can even imagine. She's going where it's Christmas every day!"

"Yeah, I know, but it's still hard. She was just gettin' her act together. I'll never forget when we talked at Piney

Hollow the night of the retreat. She really did come clean. And even the way she felt about her mom changed. She's been praying for her too."

"Yeah, I know." Morgan sighed and reached for the box again. "Just remember, we promised that we'd pray for her mom, too. God can change her heart."

"Yeah, but when? Can you believe Mrs. Bodmer hasn't come even once to see Sooze? I wonder if she even cares one little bit."

"Some people just can't handle being around sick folks. Like my family," said Morgan. "It's too scary for them. Like I said, we'll just keep praying."

"Girls," Skye heard Mrs. Chambers' voice from the living room, you better come in here."

Skye and Morgan looked into each other's eyes. Neither one said what Skye knew was in each of their hearts. It was time to say good-bye. But as they slipped into the room, they noticed that Sooze was awake. A weak smile crossed her face as she caught sight of her friends.

Mr. and Mrs. Chambers were on each side of the bed. Their eyes were swollen and red, and both of them looked like they hadn't slept in a week. Mrs. Chambers stroked Sooze's cheek gently. On a lamp table next to the bed rested a gift box with a tag labeled "Mom." A silence settled on the group, and then Sooze spoke. "She's coming. I know she is. God told me my mom is coming to say good-bye."

Skye gave Morgan a quick look and then turned her eyes back to Sooze. In only a few days, it seemed that

Sooze had faded away to almost nothing. Her head, covered with a thin layer of fuzz, highlighted her eyes that had sunken deeper into her ashen face. Her chest rose with each shallow breath and then lowered in a jerking motion.

Skye sat, staring at her friend. *This can't be real. I've got to wake up from this nightmare*, she told herself. The heaviest weight she had ever felt pressed down on her. It felt like her heart was being ripped right out of her chest. *My best friend is dying, and I can't do a thing to help her.* Skye blinked, streams of hot tears flooding her cheeks. With a sigh of disbelief, she leaned on the bed and folded her hands in front of her quivering lips.

A knock at the door, faint and unsure, broke the tearful silence. Mrs. C. brushed the tears from her face and turned toward the gentle knock. She went to the door and slowly opened it.

As Mrs. C. stood back for the guest to enter, Skye and Morgan both gasped. There before them stood a lonely figure, cold as the rush of the winter night itself.

Mrs. Chambers reached out to welcome the woman at the door, and Skye's heart leaped. She brushed back her tears and as she did, a deep inner peace made its way into the depths of her soul, a peace that only comes from God.

"Mrs. Bodmer! Come in!" Mr. C. said.

With a new-found hope in her heart, Skye turned to Sooze, who had turned her head toward her mother.

"Oh, Sooze," Skye said with excitement. "Your mother did come. Now I know God answers prayer."

Sooze smiled, and Skye thought she looked like an angel. Sooze reached out one thin, pale arm to the woman who now stood next to her bed.

Mrs. Bodmer kissed her daughter's hand as tears flowed freely from her eyes onto the bed covers.

"I love you, Mom," Sooze said.

"I know I ain't never told you, Sooze, but I love you, too. I don't know why I couldn't ever do right by you. I'm so sorry. Can you ever forgive me?"

Sooze nodded sweetly and continued to smile up into her mother's face. "I forgive you and God will forgive you too, Mom. All you have to do is ask."

A comforting presence filled the room that, without question in Skye's heart, outshone the glow of the Christmas lights. She knew her God was here. She knew there was nothing to fear.

Slowly, mustering strength from a source higher than her own, Sooze stared fixedly at the corner of the room.

"It's time for me to go now. I'm not afraid. I'll see you all again in heaven one day."

Sooze's voice was barely more than a whisper. Her lungs emptied with one long rattle, and her eyes drooped shut. Her parched lips forced upward into her last smile on Earth, one that could only mean victory!

For the next few moments, which seemed like hours, the family sat in frozen silence, hoping against hope that they might see one more breath.

Mr. Chambers' weak voice cracked, "Sooze is with the Lord."

Skye sat with her family. Their sobs intermingled with the fleeting joy of a Christmas Eve that would stay with them the rest of their lives. Mrs. Chambers stood with her arms encircling Mrs. Bodmer, comforting her in her grief. Finally, Mr. Chambers prayed, committing Sooze and their own futures into the hands of the Lord.

Someday, Skye's breaking heart declared with its own victorious shout, *someday in heaven, we'll be buds again!*

And now clearer than ever, the message of the season rang out—that Jesus Christ came to Earth that first Christmas so long ago for just this purpose—to take away the power of death.

Quietly at first, and then with gathering strength, the family began to sing *Silent Night* as a hymn of praise to God.

Glossary of Gaits

Gait–A gait is the manner of movement, the way a horse goes.

There are four natural or major gaits most horses use: walk, trot, canter, and gallop.

Walk–In the walk, the slowest gait, hooves strike the ground in a four-beat order: right hind hoof, right fore hoof, left hind hoof, left fore hoof.

Trot–In the trot, hooves strike the ground in diagonals in a one-two beat: right hind and left forefeet together, left hind and right forefeet together.

Canter–The canter is a three-beat gait containing an instant during which all four hooves are off the ground. The foreleg that lands last is called the "lead" leg and seems to point in the direction of the canter.

Gallop–The gallop is the fastest gait. If fast enough, it's a four-beat gait, with each hoof landing separately: right hind hoof, left hind hoof just before right fore hoof, left fore hoof.

Other gaits come naturally to certain breeds or are developed through careful breeding.

Running walk–This smooth gait comes naturally to the Tennessee walking horse. The horse glides between a walk and a trot.

Pace–A two-beat gait, similar to a trot. But instead of legs pairing in diagonals as in the trot, fore and hindlegs on one side move together, giving a swaying action.

Slow gait–Four beats, but with swaying from side to side and a prancing effect. The slow gait is one of the gaits used by Five-Gaited Saddle Horses. Some call this pace the stepping pace or amble.

Amble–A slow, easy gait, much like the pace.

Rack–One of the five gaits of the Five-Gaited American Saddle Horse, it's a fancy, fast walk. This four-beat gait is faster than the trot and is very hard on the horse.

Jog–A jog is a slow trot, sometimes called a *dogtrot.*

Lope–A slow, easygoing canter, usually referring to a western gait on a horse ridden with loose reins.

Fox trot–An easy gait of short steps in which the horse basically walks in front and trots behind. It's a smooth gait, great for long-distance riding and characteristic of the Missouri Fox Trotter.

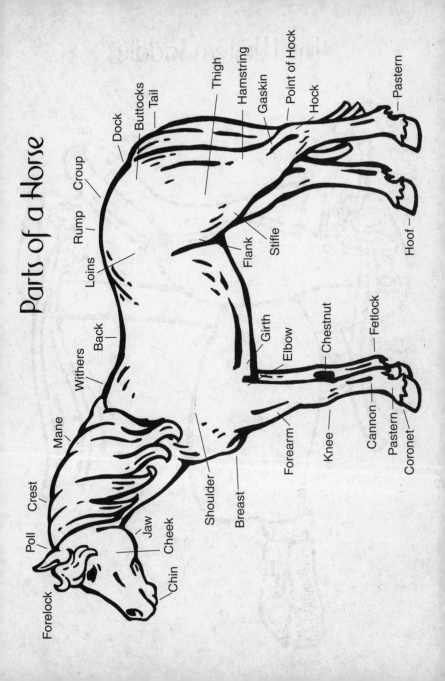

Parts of a Horse

Poll
Crest
Forelock
Mane
Jaw
Cheek
Chin
Withers
Back
Loins
Rump
Croup
Dock
Buttocks
Tail
Thigh
Hamstring
Gaskin
Point of Hock
Hock
Pastern
Stifle
Flank
Girth
Elbow
Chestnut
Fetlock
Cannon
Pastern
Coronet
Knee
Forearm
Breast
Shoulder
Hoof

The Western Saddle

Horn

Gullet
(underside)

Concho

Swell

Cantle

Seat

Jockey

Rear
Housing

Skirt

Latigo
Carrier

Strings

Rigging
Ring

Fender

Stirrup

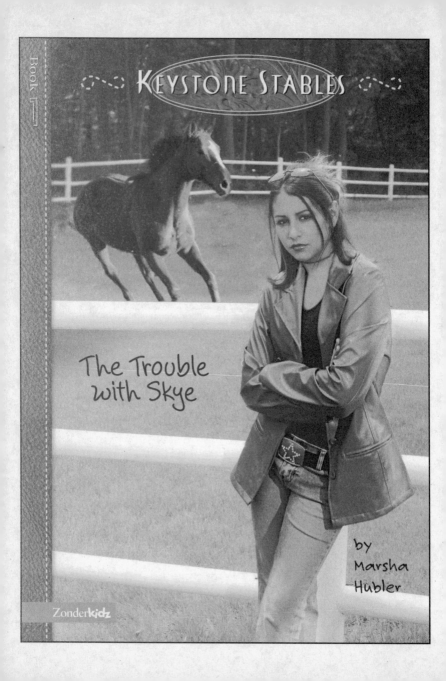

The Trouble with Skye
(Book 1)
Written by Marsha Hubler

Thirteen-year-old foster kid Skye Nicholson has become an expert at being an angry, cold, and defensive teenager. She's been through so much and committed so many offenses that she knows with her last antic, she's on her last leg. After breaking five foster home placements, she's headed to her final resort—juvenile detention.

But suddenly, hope finds her through the tough love of Tom and Eileen Chambers, who offer her another chance in their home. They introduce her to a God that has the power to truly save her, no matter how much she thinks she's not worth saving.

Softcover 0-310-70572-X

Available now at your local bookstore!

Zonderkidz

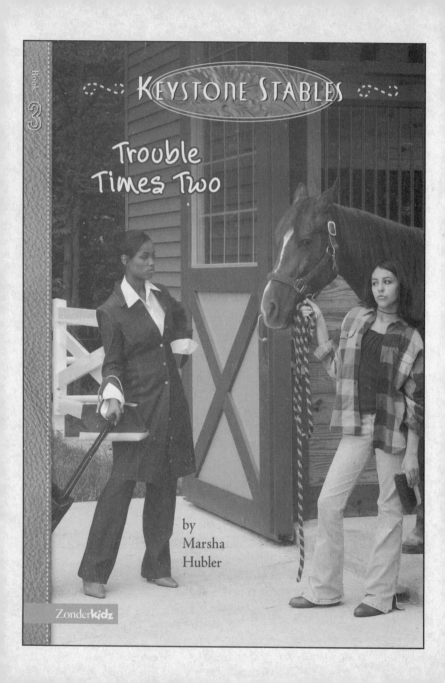

Trouble Times Two
(Book 3)
Written by Marsha Hubler

Skye and Morgan have their hands full trying to share
both God's love and life's most precious qualities with
Tanya Bell, a runaway who becomes a foster child in the
Chambers' household. Despite the fact that her adoptive
mother is a wealthy physician and gives her everything,
Tanya is a veteran shoplifter. The introspective Tanya
wrestles with her past; however, when one of the mares
dies giving birth to a foal, Tanya is forced to face the very
person she could never run away from—herself.

Softcover 0-310-70574-6

Coming soon to your local bookstore!

Zonderkidz

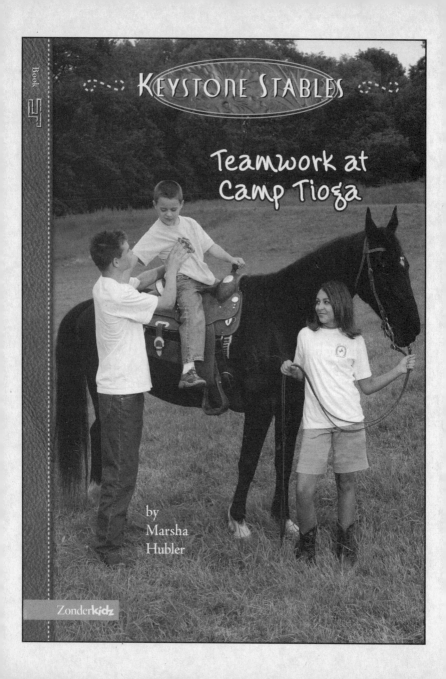

KEYSTONE STABLES

Teamwork at Camp Tioga

by
Marsha
Hubler

Zonderkidz

Coming
Spring 2005

Teamwork at Camp Tioga
(Book 4)
Written by Marsha Hubler

Skye is so excited to work as a teen counselor at a special needs camp, especially when she discovers that Chad Dressler is also working there. Her heart races every time she sees him, but the thrill is short-lived when one of the non-hearing campers starts causing havoc during his riding lessons. Skye takes a crash course in American Sign Language to try to communicate with him, but to no avail—he's still too stubborn. When he disappears on horseback into the hills, it's up to Skye and Chad to lead the rescue mission.

Softcover 0-310-70575-4

Coming soon to your local bookstore!

Zonderkidz

We want to hear from you. Please send your comments about this book to us in care of zreview@zondervan.com. Thank you.

Zonder**kidz**®

Grand Rapids, MI 49530
www.zonderkidz.com